# Praise for the Safe Harbor Medical ® Mysteries

## *The Case of the Questionable Quadruplet*

"Love the mystery and medical setting interwoven to tell a great story. Lots of twists and turns and plenty of suspects. The end is unexpected and the reveal compelling."
—Sandy Penny, SweetMysteryBooks.blogspot.com

"This is a wonderfully written mystery with lots of twists and turns that kept me glued to the book."
—Online Reviewer Jo-Anne B

## *The Case of the Surly Surrogate*

"A very clever mystery where emotions and feelings ran deep making for a truly beautiful read."
—Pauline Michael, NightOwlReviews

"Attention cozy mystery readers: Jacqueline Diamond's second Safe Harbor Medical mystery only gets better! 5 Stars."
—Mary Castillo, author of *Lost in the Light*

## *The Case of the Desperate Doctor*

"The mystery progresses at a swift speed and keeps you engaged with likable characters."
—Tracy Farnsworth, *Round Table Reviews*

## Books by Jacqueline Diamond

### Safe Harbor Medical ® Mysteries

THE CASE OF THE QUESTIONABLE QUADRUPLET

THE CASE OF THE SURLY SURROGATE

THE CASE OF THE DESPERATE DOCTOR

THE CASE OF THE LONG-LOST LOVER

### More Mysteries and Suspense

AND THE BRIDE VANISHES

DANGER MUSIC

ECHOES

HIS SECRET SON

THE EYES OF A STRANGER

TOUCH ME IN THE DARK

### Safe Harbor Medical ® Romances

THE WOULD-BE MOMMY

HIS HIRED BABY

THE HOLIDAY TRIPLETS

OFFICER DADDY

FALLING FOR THE NANNY

THE SURGEON'S SURPRISE TWINS

THE DETECTIVE'S ACCIDENTAL BABY

THE BABY DILEMMA

THE M.D.'S SECRET DAUGHTER

THE BABY JACKPOT

HIS BABY DREAM

The Case of the

DESPERATE DOCTOR

Safe Harbor Medical ® Mysteries

Book Three

# Jacqueline Diamond

Published by K. Loren Wilson

P.O. Box 1315, Brea, California, USA

*The Case of the Desperate Doctor*, copyright © 2018 by Jackie Diamond Hyman

Cover art copyright © 2019 by Jackie Diamond Hyman

Safe Harbor Medical ® is a trademark registered with the U.S. Patent and Trademark Office by Jackie Diamond Hyman

For subsidiary rights, please contact the author at jdiamondfriends@yahoo.com or P.O. Box 1315, Brea, Calif. 92822.

More information about the books and the author is available at www.jacquelinediamond.net.

ISBN-13: 978-1-936505-64-7
ISBN-10-1936505649

# From the Author

Although I work alone on my ideas, character development, plotting and writing, the process of completing a novel also requires research, editing and feedback. I'm grateful for the input of friends, fellow authors and subject experts.

For his invaluable advice, I want to thank Orange County Sheriff's Investigator Gary Bale (retired). I'm also grateful to my Beta readers, Deborah Golub R.N., Brooke Hamilton, Marcia Holman R.N., and Amanda Luna Joya, and my critique group, Orange County Fictionaires. Also, a tip of the hat to D.P. Lyle, M.D., novelist and forensics expert, who answers complicated questions quickly and thoroughly.

Welcome to the third Safe Harbor Medical Mystery!

Jacqueline Diamond
Brea, California
2018

In memory of my father,

Maurice Schwartz Hyman, M.D.

# CHAPTER ONE

"I think I might have killed her."

It takes a lot to stop a forkful of food from reaching my mouth. Around me, the noise of the hospital cafeteria faded and, with a bite of chicken poised in midair, I focused on the rangy, dark-haired man seated across the table.

Like me, Dr. Jeremiah Schwartz was an obstetrician-gynecologist. Unlike me, he was a card-carrying weirdo and, for me personally, a decades-long annoyance who imitated me at every step. Among recent developments, he'd bought a car identical to mine, leased an office near mine in the medical building next to the hospital, and taken it upon himself to join me for lunch whenever possible. His unpredictable comments ranged from intriguing to, as had just occurred, bizarre.

There was little doubt who "she" referred to. On this Tuesday afternoon, the staff was abuzz with word that Dr. Alison Abrams had been found dead in her bathtub the previous day, and with speculation as to whether her death had been an accident or suicide. The police were, as usual, keeping a lid on the investigation.

An ob-gyn with admitting privileges here at Safe Harbor Medical Center, Alison had maintained a private office in nearby Newport Beach. Until about a year and a half earlier, Jeremiah had worked with her and another doctor. Other than that, I wasn't aware of any connection between them.

As I mulled his statement, my fork resumed its journey to my mouth. The absence of others at our table was fortunate. They might have overreacted, or else considered this a bad joke. Jeremiah never joked.

He frowned. "Did you hear me, Eric?"

"Why do you think you killed her?" I asked.

"She showed up at my apartment Saturday night." Jeremiah pushed aside his plate and folded his bony hands on the table.

"Alison did?"

"Yes. Without advance notice. I was unaware of her plans, such as they were."

"What plans?"

"To have sex with me."

Although unsure I wished to hear this, I couldn't resist inquiring, "And did you?"

He coughed. "Yes."

I pictured Alison's tall, athletic figure and strong face, the light-brown hair pulled into a bun. She'd carried a lot of tension in her jaw, holding in things she couldn't or wouldn't say. She'd been around forty, three years older than me. Although we'd inhabited the same world professionally, we'd had no mutual friends, to my knowledge.

"Had this happened before?" I asked.

"We had never previously slept together." Although he grew up in New York, Jeremiah spoke English as if it were his second language. He'd done that as long as I'd known him, which was since we both attended Harvard Medical School. "I did not understand her motivation."

"For sleeping with you?" Although I'd avoided entanglements since my wife's death three years earlier, most single men seemed to leap at the chance for a hookup. They rarely questioned the woman's motives.

"Correct. I could not read her mood," Jeremiah said. "However, I can rarely read anyone's mood, except when they are angry. She was not."

His mood-reading abilities were none of my concern. Nor was his visit from Alison, since the timing appeared to render this tryst irrelevant to her death. "Did you see her on Sunday, too?"

"She did not stay over," he said.

"She was alive and ambulatory when she left on Saturday night?" I glanced at the cafeteria clock. About twenty minutes remained until my afternoon appointments.

"Yes. Do you find it odd that she departed immediately after we had sex? I rarely sleep with women," he added.

This uninvited disclosure raised a question I had never asked and had no desire to pose now, because the answer might ignite something dark and dangerous inside me. While we were in medical school, my longtime girlfriend, my soulmate and later wife, Lydia, had taken a break from our relationship. During that period, she'd dated Jeremiah, although in my opinion they'd had nothing in common aside from being grandchildren of Holocaust survivors. After a month, she'd broken it off and returned to me.

Although Lydia and I had been each other's closest friends since our freshman year in high school, there were things I didn't know about her. One of them was whether she'd slept with the man opposite me.

After she ended their association, she'd shown no further interest in him. Jeremiah, however, had fixated on her and, by extension, on me. When Lydia and I moved back to Southern California, he'd applied to the same residency program and followed us here. He imitated my clothing choices, got his hair cut by the same barber and had twice bought cars identical to mine, even special-ordering the color.

However, according to my friend Keith, a police detective, Jeremiah's actions fell short of stalking. He issued no threats, hadn't harassed either of us and, as far as Lydia and I could determine, hadn't staked out our house.

Jeremiah must have guessed my line of thought from my expression. As he'd indicated, he could detect anger. "I did not sleep with Lydia," he said. "At least, I do not believe so."

"You what?' I shot to my feet, rattling the dishes. Around us, people stared, and conversations paused. I didn't give a damn. "How could you *not* remember?"

"Please sit down," Jeremiah replied. "You are drawing attention. This outburst is not characteristic of you, Eric."

Recalling that patients might be dining here, I sat. The hum of voices gradually resumed. "Well?"

He struggled to speak, as if afraid of what he might reveal or how I would react. Strange, considering he'd practically confessed to murder.

Jeremiah's gaze grew distant, and then it cleared, as if he had applied mental windshield wipers. "I am not always certain if what I see has truly occurred."

I'd disliked this man for over a decade, scoffed at his eccentricities and resented his intrusions. Although I'd considered he might be on the autism spectrum, that had not resolved my questions. At this instant, his symptoms finally presented me with a diagnosis.

"You're schizophrenic," I said

He nodded, almost in relief.

With proper treatment, a schizophrenic doctor can function effectively, as Jeremiah did. To my knowledge, he handled his cases adequately and hadn't been sued any more than the rest of us. You'd think a bunch of doctors would recognize the symptoms, but some of us are real oddballs to begin with. "Are you on medication?"

"I am," he said. "My psychiatrist states that I am doing well."

"So well that you aren't sure whether you killed Alison?" I kept my voice low.

"My hallucinations can be very real, and logic is my yardstick," Jeremiah explained. "It is irrational to believe she appeared at my apartment and requested sex. I did discover a hair clip in my bathroom that might be hers. If she was actually there, I need to determine the connection to her death, if any."

"You aren't certain what happened last weekend," I summarized. "In spite of taking antipsychotic meds."

"My disease does not have an off-switch," he replied. "More of a dimmer. There are transient thoughts that fail the logic test immediately. That I burned down my apartment building, for example, or that there are egrets flocking in the hallway."

"How about the delusion that you've killed someone?"

"I do not recall murdering Alison," Jeremiah said. "I merely consider it a possibility."

"Why tell me about it?" I asked.

He spread his hands, indicating the answer should be obvious. "For the past decade, you have served as my touchstone to reality. Were you not aware of this?"

"No." I was both fascinated and disturbed. "In what sense am I your touchstone?"

"I will not bore you with the history of my illness," Jeremiah said. "Except that, following a couple of breakdowns, concentration on my studies anchored me. However, the future after medical school threatened chaos. Already, I struggled to pass as normal. How could I function without the framework of school?"

"How indeed?" Around us, staff members were finishing their meals, drinking their umpteenth cups of coffee for the day, and toting trays to the conveyer belt. Cafeteria workers in yellow uniforms collected dishes left by the inconsiderate, while outside on the patio, visible through glass doors, a few hardy souls dined beneath heat lamps against the February chill.

Everything was normal except at this table, where I sat mesmerized. Only an urgent summons by phone could have dislodged me. For once, none came.

"When I saw that Lydia preferred you to me, I observed that others respected you, also," Jeremiah continued. "I concluded that if I chose you as my pattern, I would be accepted."

"That's why you decided to be an ob-gyn and applied for a residency here?"

"Of course," he said. "And everything else."

He hadn't been fixated on my wife. He'd clung to me as a plumb line, a guide to staying vertical in a world with an ever-shifting horizon.

I didn't want to care about Jeremiah, who'd been a stone in my shoe for ages. Recently, to be fair, he had warmed up a little. I credited this to the influence of his nurse, a pleasant young woman who admired him, unlike her string of predecessors. But I had no interest in serving as either his pattern or his support.

Nevertheless, no one deserves to suffer from a devastating disease, and schizophrenia is near the top of my list. During its active phase, the brain disorder may bring on overwhelming delusions and confused thinking. Some people recover completely for long periods or even permanently but, if not, it can disrupt lives and short-circuit careers.

As long as I could remember, I had been driven to protect the suffering. This sense of obligation intensified after I lost my wife. Lydia's death in a fall had been declared accidental, but to me it remained mysterious, as was her withdrawal from me in the preceding months.

Jeremiah's willingness to confide what was evidently a closely guarded secret, and to trust me with his fear of what he might have done to Alison, imposed a moral obligation, whether I desired it or not. Okay, not. But it existed, nevertheless.

His next question was, "Eric, what should I do?"

My mind skittered across what I'd read about Alison's death. When she'd failed to arrive at her office and couldn't be reached, her nurse had gone to her home and discovered her body in the tub. Today's *Safe Harbor Journal* hadn't indicated whether she'd drowned or if there'd been a suicide note, only that she'd died late Sunday or very early Monday. The police were treating the death as suspicious, according to the article.

*Had* someone killed Alison? In recent years, murder had claimed several people close to me. Each case had an eerie way of sending ripples through the universe that intersected with my life.

None of this explained why she would have arrived at Jeremiah's apartment on Saturday expecting intercourse, when they had no history of sexual involvement. Unless, of course, he'd hallucinated it.

*So, Doc, what should he do? Go to the police?*

The hair clip aside, there was no proof that she'd visited Jeremiah. He'd never struck me as dangerous. Moreover, contact with the police might lead to public disclosure of his mental illness, harming his medical practice without justification.

"I'm not an attorney and, if you really believe you're implicated, you should hire one," I began.

"Is that what you would do?" he asked.

I hadn't volunteered to serve as his template. Still, after his confidence, it seemed unfair to insist that whatever I might choose was none of his business. I provided an honest answer. "Unless I remembered anything that might help in the investigation, I'd keep it to myself."

He released a long breath. "I am glad."

So was I. For about a minute.

That's when a blond, broad-shouldered man—former high school football player, owner of a red sports car, who might have flunked junior high math without my tutoring—strode into the cafeteria. Head high, shoulders straight, exuding what's termed command presence, homicide detective Keith Sparks surveyed the room.

We rarely saw police at our hospital, since it has no emergency room. And my friend didn't pay social calls on a work day. In any case, he skimmed right over me and focused on the thin, elongated figure of Jeremiah.

Keith headed toward us.

# CHAPTER TWO

"Dr. Jeremiah Schwartz?" When my companion rose, our visitor said, "I'm Detective Keith Sparks."

"You are Eric's friend," Jeremiah replied as they shook hands. At six-foot-three, the doctor topped the policeman by a few inches. However, in a confrontation, I'd bet on the lion over the giraffe.

Around us, the departing diners slowed their pace. I pictured a cafeteria full of mimes, pretending to run while barely moving.

"I'd like to ask you a few questions at the station."

Jeremiah didn't bother with "why?" or "what's this about?" He said, "I would be happy to respond to your inquiries, detective, but I have patients waiting. So does Dr. Darcy."

"What does Eric have to do with this?" There was an edge to Keith's voice. Normally, despite a short fuse in private life, he exuded cool objectivity with witnesses. I was aware of this because I'd had occasion to view him in this mode before.

"The interview will take place at 6:00 p.m., if you are free. I recommend a neutral site such as the conference room in our office building next door," Jeremiah said. "I will be accompanied either by an attorney or by Eric, if he is available."

Keith's jaw worked. He preferred to interview his suspects and witnesses, or whatever he considered Jeremiah, alone.

"I can be there." Curiosity as much as any newfound loyalty prompted my consent. I didn't bother to add that I was in no position to provide legal advice. In addition to the usual smarts required to complete medical training, Jeremiah had done so while fighting phantoms in his brain. He didn't need mothering.

"It's important for my investigation to proceed quickly," Keith said.

"A few hours will not change the facts," Jeremiah said. "Are we agreed on the time and place?"

"Fine with me," I said.

Keith acquiesced less than happily.

"I shall see you both then." Jeremiah retrieved his tray and merged into the accelerating flow of fellow staffers.

"What the hell?" Keith muttered. "I don't get this guy. Especially why he's dragging you into it."

He'd heard me complain often enough about Jeremiah, and it was tempting to explain what I'd just learned about serving as the man's model. Tempting, but a violation of my colleague's trust.

"You'd rather it was me than an attorney," I said.

"Obviously."

"The conference room's on the sixth floor. See you."

Keith growled what might have been a farewell.

Why was he interested in Jeremiah? I wondered as I exited the hospital and strolled  to the adjacent building. Had there been more between Jeremiah and Alison than he'd revealed? Was it possible he could be violent and not remember?

*Slow down.* It wasn't established that anyone had murdered Alison. Also, this might be nothing more on Keith's part than checking him out as a former coworker.

My practice, which I'd inherited from my father, occupied an office on the fourth floor of the medical building. I'd also inherited his partner, Dr. Isaiah Levin, who was in his early seventies.

When I entered my suite from the hall via a side door, I heard the hum of voices in the waiting room. My nurse, Farrah, greeted me with the information that we had to accommodate more than the usual number of extra patients, since I'd been in surgery all morning and Isaiah took off Tuesday afternoons to play golf.

After asking the receptionist, Glenda, to reserve the conference room in case that didn't occur to Jeremiah, I scanned the first patient's face sheet and banished everything else from my mind. Well, almost. At odd moments during the afternoon, I couldn't avoid hearing updates. While Glenda handled her duties responsibly, she scanned social media and kept up on the news during lulls.

"They located Dr. Abrams' car a couple of miles from her house," the young woman announced breathlessly, brown curls bouncing. "Why do you suppose she parked that far away? There must have been monkey business."

"Or it broke and hadn't been towed yet," Farrah said.

I declined to speculate.

"Her poor nurse," Glenda went on. "What a shock to stumble across her body. And what about their patients?"

Alison's medical partner, Chuck Kane, was no doubt figuring out the logistics at a frantic pace. I didn't envy him.

By six o'clock, I'd wrapped my caseload and determined that none of my patients was in labor. Since Safe Harbor's staff included an obstetrician on regular overnight duty, I rarely got called in after hours. However, I did my best to stay available for emergencies.

The elevator opened to reveal a sole occupant. Legs apart,

his suit rumpled in back as reflected in the mirror, Keith stood glaring forward. I didn't take it personally. He liked being in control and this was my territory and Jeremiah's, not his.

"Tell me one thing," he said after the doors closed.

"Shoot."

"What do you think of this guy?" Undoubtedly, he meant the Jeremiah. "Is he for real?"

Carefully, I said, "I've never known him to be anything other than flat-out honest. I'm not sure he's capable of deceit, although from your viewpoint, I'm sure everyone is."

"Damn straight," he said.

On the sixth floor, I guided Keith to the conference room. En route, he scowled at a man in a suit who was exiting an orthopedist's office.

"He's not a lawyer," I muttered as the man limped toward the elevator.

"How do you know?"

"Not a relevant lawyer," I corrected.

My friend's tension didn't ease until we entered the conference room and saw Jeremiah alone at the long table, wearing a white lab coat. He'd placed a water pitcher and three glasses conveniently close.

Behind him, a row of tinted windows provided a panoramic view over the bluffs. Below spread a beach lapped by the Pacific and, to our left, the small-boat harbor from which the town takes its name. In the twilight, the only thing stirring was traffic along Pacific Coast Highway.

Jeremiah produced his phone. "You do not object to my recording the interview?"

That would be wise for anyone, I reflected. Doubly so for a man uncertain that his memories were factual.

"I plan to do that as well." Keith removed a recorder from his briefcase, plus a pad and pen. When we were settled, he checked the sound level, gave the date, time and location, and asked each of us to state our name.

"Dr. Eric Darcy." I felt like I was addressing an audience.

"Dr. Jeremiah Schwartz."

"Detective Keith Sparks. Dr. Darcy is observing at Dr. Schwartz's insistence." He fixed me with a stare. "You will simply observe. Is that understood?"

"Absolutely." I sat back to listen.

What was the nature of Jeremiah's relationship to Dr. Alison Abrams? He related their history, and explained that he'd left to launch a solo practice when an office became available in this building.

Keith asked whether he kept drugs in the office.

"Prenatal vitamins," Jeremiah said. "A few other samples from manufacturers."

"Anything for anxiety or depression?"

"No."

That raised the issue, to me, of whether Alison had swallowed an overdose. While I was mulling that notion, Keith picked up his previous topic. "Was there more to your relationship with Dr. Abrams than a professional association?"

"Not until Saturday night," Jeremiah said.

An eyelid twitched. "What happened then?"

"We had sex."

Another twitch. "Where was that?"

"At my apartment," Jeremiah said.

"So we would have no reason to find your DNA at her house?" Keith asked.

That startled me. *Had* Jeremiah been at her home? Or was he fishing?

"Only if Alison transferred it there. If she did, it should be minimal." Jeremiah sipped his water before continuing. "Tell me, detective, have the police been watching me?"

13

"What?" It was Keith's turn to be caught off guard.

"I believe you were already aware that Alison visited me on Saturday night," he said. "Is that not correct?"

"Why would you think we'd been watching you?" Keith countered.

I struggled to keep up with this ping-pong match. If the subject were less serious, it might have been entertaining.

"Paranoia," Jeremiah replied. "However, I suspect that my snoopy landlady contacted you after Alison's picture appeared on the news." To me, he noted, "Mrs. Linden observes the neighborhood with spyglasses. I believe she has entered my premises several times without permission and opened my drawers."

"Why do you stay there?" I asked.

He shrugged. "The rent is reasonable. Besides, everybody needs a hobby."

Keith narrowed his eyes at me. *Stay out of this, buddy.* "Tell me what happened Saturday night," he said.

Jeremiah repeated his account of Alison arriving and requesting sex. And leaving that same night, unharmed.

"Did she say what her plans were?" Keith asked.

"She did not."

"Did she seem upset or depressed?"

"Not to me." Jeremiah had the good sense to make his answers short and on target. No reference to his inability to read moods.

"Dr. Schwartz, where were you Sunday night between ten p.m. and one a.m.?" Translation: *Do you have an alibi?*

"Home alone. Hopefully, Mrs. Linden can confirm that." Jeremiah's eyebrows pinched together. "Unless I went out."

"*Did* you?" Keith asked.

"I am fairly certain I did not."

I imagined how a detective might take this. As a sign that

the witness was covering his bases, should anyone have seen him? Or...

"Dr. Schwartz, do you drink heavily?" Keith asked.

"I never consume alcohol," Jeremiah said.

"Did Dr. Abrams?"

"Not in my presence," he said.

Through the window, the last hints of sunset faded into darkness. "Did she use drugs?" Keith asked.

"Not that I observed." Jeremiah's expression remained calm. What was his inner screen showing him? Perhaps his concentration was holding the phantoms at bay.

"And you, Dr. Schwartz?"

"I take prescription medication," he said.

"What sort of prescription medication?" Keith pursued.

Jeremiah hesitated only a tick before responding. "Antipsychotic medication for schizophrenia."

That knocked Keith into several seconds of silence before he asked, "That's why you mentioned paranoia?"

"I am only mildly paranoid, but yes," Jeremiah said.

*And that's why he wasn't sure whether he went out on Sunday,* I nearly added.

"You see a psychiatrist?"

He nodded.

"Which one?"

I didn't consider the details of my colleague's medical treatment any of the police's business. However, Jeremiah was entitled to disclose it if he wished.

"Dr. Boris Norton. His office is in Anaheim," Jeremiah said.

"Did you ever consult a psychiatrist named Ward Radman?"

Why him, specifically? I wondered.

Jeremiah took the question in stride. "No. But I presume Dr. Abrams' nurse has advised you."

*Of what?*

15

"Please elaborate," When Keith relaxed the grip on his pen, it left red marks on his fingers.

My brain galloped ahead. Had Alison been undergoing treatment? Had someone over prescribed medication or endangered her by failing to account for other drugs in her system? Many medications amplify, alter or block the effects of others. The results can be lethal.

However, Keith wasn't discussing an ordinary psychiatrist. Radio host and author Ward Radman had addressed hospital staff recently as part of our Medical Insight Series. He cultivated a reputation for promoting understanding of and respect for people with nonmainstream sexual identities, the LGBTQ community. His lecture on issues facing lesbians, gays, bisexuals, transsexuals and those who prefer the term "queers" had been informative, and peppered with lively anecdotes.

It had also been annoying. Not because of the subject; my patients include lesbians and transsexuals. However, Radman's primary qualification as an authority was his ability to showboat. I mistrust experts whose goal strikes me more as self-promotion than either compassion or the advancement of science.

A large man, Radman possessed a ready smile and a thin skin. Charming, quick-witted and manipulative, he'd fired back instantly at any audience comment that might be perceived as criticism.

Later, I'd scanned his bestselling book, *OnWard, UpWard! Loving Your Sexual Identity*. It regurgitated information widely available, such as how to handle coming out to your friends and relatives. He also promoted himself and his subject on a radio show and video/audio podcasts.

Jeremiah's words broke into my reflections. "Dr. Radman mentored Alison during her academic career." The psychiatrist had been on the faculty at California Southstate University in the inland town of Azalea Springs during Alison's premed years, he said, and served as her adviser in medical school.

"At a later point, he behaved in a manner that offended her," Jeremiah added. "Once when his name was mentioned, she reacted angrily. Nurse Cornello might have more information."

Keith jotted a note. Since Brandy Cornello had, according to the news, discovered Alison's body, I assumed she'd already been interviewed.

"Do you believe the offense was of a sexual nature?" Keith asked.

"I do not care to speculate."

More inquiries followed, occasionally backtracking or lurching out of the blue, as if to throw Jeremiah off his game. Did Alison mention Dr. Radman on Saturday night? No. Did Jeremiah have reason to believe she'd visited other men seeking sex? No. What reason had she given for suddenly seeking a tryst? She had not explained, Jeremiah said. How would he describe Alison's house? He could not, since he'd never seen it. Nothing threw him off his game because, in my opinion, there was no game.

Keith inquired further about schizophrenia and its effects. Jeremiah spoke frankly about the bizarre images and thoughts, which he equated to a nightmare from which it is impossible to awaken.

"Yet, you can function as a doctor?"

"I can. I do. You may ask Dr. Darcy."

"He does," I volunteered.

Keith avoided looking at me. If he had, I suspected he'd have rolled his eyes at my simplistic statement.

"Is there anything else I should be aware of?" Keith asked his subject.

"Nothing springs to mind."

The interview concluded with a request that Jeremiah remain available. He solemnly consented. Keith ended the recording with a statement of the time, place and who was present.

As we rose, I visualized us all three of us exiting simultaneously, with awkward attempts to pass through the doorway and down the hall, getting stuck shoulder-to-shoulder in the process. Instead, after a brief hesitation, Keith took his leave.

Did he expect me to repeat anything Jeremiah might confide afterward? If it were significant, I'd be obliged to. Withholding important data might implicate me as an accessory after the fact.

When my colleague said, "There is another matter I have not told you," my chest tightened.

"Should we ask Keith to come back?"

"This does not concern Detective Sparks," Jeremiah said. "It is about Lydia."

My late wife? He had my full attention. "What about her?"

"Alison was treating her at our office," he said.

My wife had always preferred a primary care doctor to a specialist for checkups. I wasn't aware that she'd consulted an ob-gyn. "When and why?"

"About three years ago." On his feet, Jeremiah towered over the conference table. "I do not have the details."

I waited. He remained silent. "That's it?"

"I thought it might be of interest," he said.

"Thank you."

I headed downstairs in a storm of thoughts. Why had my wife decided to visit an ob-gyn, and why hadn't she mentioned it to me?

For many months after her death, I'd attributed Lydia's coolness to a discussion about children. After a night of delivering and holding newborns, I'd revealed a powerful desire for fatherhood. We'd never seriously discussed children before that, although we'd been best friends since we were little more than kids ourselves.

Although she hadn't argued, her withdrawal began soon afterwards. Much later, however, I'd learned from a friend of hers that Lydia had wanted children, too. That hadn't been the reason for what had bordered on an estrangement.

Was her visit to Alison significant? If she'd decided we should start planning a family, why keep me in the dark? Since I hadn't run across any mention of a physician in the paperwork I'd sorted as her executor, it had never occurred to me to seek her medical records.

*Why didn't you trust me, Lydia?* Now Jeremiah had handed me a key to a door I hadn't known existed.

Distractedly, I traced the path to the parking structure. I'd left my champagne-colored electric car at a charging station next to its twin, property of the absent Jeremiah.

As I drove out of the medical complex, a commercial replaced the music on my radio. Channel switching, I caught the glib voice of Dr. Ward Radman, which—thanks to his radio program and podcasts—was difficult to escape these days.

I was about to shut it off. Then I realized he was talking about Alison.

# CHAPTER THREE

How, I wondered as I headed south toward the ocean in the early-evening darkness, could anyone listen to Dr. Ward Radman without detecting the smugness and phoniness that infused his cultivated tones? Vast swathes of the public must lack the ability to detect guile, to the eternal enrichment of con artists.

*Shut up, brain. Pay attention.*

"Like many of you, I experienced shock on hearing that Newport Beach obstetrician Alison Abrams killed herself," the psychiatrist related, as if her suicide were an established fact. "My distress was intensified because I knew her personally. In fact, as I have informed the police, I spoke with Dr. Abrams Sunday evening, when she arrived at my home unexpectedly."

I hit the brake hard as a red light loomed. Behind me, a large truck honked. "Pay attention, buddy," I muttered, channeling my inner Keith.

"She spoke in a rambling fashion, exhibiting signs of drug or alcohol use and extreme anxiety. Because I mentored her during her education, Dr. Abrams turned to me when she felt troubled," Radman continued.

What an arrogant prick, to speak as if Alison's death was all about him. I instinctively suspected Radman of lying, or at least spinning the situation to his advantage.

Still, I did believe his statement that she'd paid him a visit. No doubt the police already knew or suspected that she'd been there, so he lost nothing by revealing it publicly. Had she asked for sex as she did with Jeremiah the previous night? Maybe she *had* been suffering a breakdown.

"There is a natural tendency, when tragedy strikes a dear one, to blame ourselves," the psychiatrist intoned. Ah, this must be the takeaway for his listeners. "Since learning of this tragedy, I've asked myself if I could have prevented it. How could I have reached out to Dr. Abrams? Yet, when I offered advice, she stormed out in such agitation that she walked home, leaving her car outside my house."

That must have been where her car ended up. Good way to cover his ass. But if she'd died at his place and he'd moved her body, wouldn't he have also moved her car? Why leave it in a spot that might implicate him?

Whatever further self-serving lessons he preached, I missed them, because the next thing I registered was, "This is Dr. Ward Radman and you've been listening to 'OnWard, UpWard! Loving Your Sexual Identity.' "

A commercial for life insurance followed.

From the boulevard, I navigated by instinct to my street. Sunset Circle lies along the bluffs above the harbor, of which my house on the inland side has a sliver of a view. Three stories tall, in the dark-timbered, multi-paned style known as Tudor Revival, it had outlived my parents and my wife and was likely to outlive me.

*You're in a great mood, Eric.*

In the broad driveway, a white van proclaimed in dark-brown lettering: Golden Fine Foods Catering. Lydia's stepfather, Morris Golden, must have finished his rounds of delivering specialty meals to customers.

When the garage door lifted, the presence of a green sedan revealed that Lydia's half-sister, Tory, was home as well. By nature, I enjoy solitude, but I could tolerate sharing a house with my in-laws as long as we maintained separate spheres.

While I collected my briefcase, I tried to collect my thoughts as well. They were full of questions about doctors Abrams and Radman. What was the real story? How had he offended her, as Jeremiah had noted, and what role had he played in her demise?

A deep breath centered me. This investigation was none of my business. Except that it seemed linked, however indirectly, to Lydia.

I entered from the garage. To my right opened the great room, where the sofas and armchairs shrank beneath the triple-height ceiling and grand curving staircase. To my left lay the open kitchen, from which issued the appetizing scents of baked cheese and spices.

On the table, a plate awaited me, featuring a large sandwich of—safe guess— gluten-free bread, stuffed with sprouty things and cheese substitute. It was accompanied by prettily carved raw vegetables and a side of hummus. As the world's worst cook, I'm grateful for my father-in-law's delivery leftovers, but I often prefer his culinary experiments such as the one currently in progress.

Morris, a chubby fellow with wisps of gray hair above his ears, removed a baking sheet from one of the double ovens and set it on the stove to cool. The pastry puffs atop parchment paper exuded heavenly aromas that held me captive until my sister-in-law, her laptop open on the counter, pierced my hunger fog by asking, "How'd it go with Keith?"

I hesitated, torn between "What smells so delicious and can I have some?" and the more flat-footed, "How did you know I was meeting with Keith?"

Tory, by the way, bears almost no resemblance to my late wife—five-ten where her older half-sister was short, crowned by a reddish-brown tumble rather than a nearly black mane—and has a brisk manner that reflects her former status as a police officer. During her ten years on the force, she rose to the rank of detective, moved in with Keith and detonated when she caught him cheating.

In the aftermath, she began a new career as a private investigator and left their apartment for my spare bedroom. Later, she conscripted my front conservatory as her office.

"Keith tells you what he's up to?" I asked After two years apart, they'd established a tolerant if wary relationship. However, I doubted he would discuss an investigation with her.

"Ran into him this afternoon at the courthouse." Both Tory and Keith occasionally testified in cases. "Bought him coffee. It's deductible."

"Ah." She was always sniffing the air for potential business. Defense attorneys as well as parties in civil cases may require the services of snoops such as her and, although her agency assigned jobs, she earned more when she brought in clients. While Keith wouldn't refer people to her, he figured into a network that helped her stay current.

"He grumbled about my interfering brother-in-law." Her husky voice reminded me of Lydia's. "I assumed you were sticking your nose into the death of that doctor."

"Good guess." *Interfering brother-in-law.* Exactly the phrasing my old pal would use when aggravated. Having heard enough on that topic, I focused on Morris. "What are those? Need a taste-tester?"

"Yes, yes." He rubbed a floury hand over his thick eyebrows. Since they were already salt-and-peppery, it caused little visible change. "Do try one. I won't name the key ingredient except that it receives far too little respect."

This might have been a danger signal. I'm a brave fellow, though, where food is concerned, as long as it isn't wild mushrooms.

"And they're called?" I asked, reaching for one.

"*Gougères.*"

"What's a goo-share?"

"You tell me."

I took a large bite. Talk about a pop of flavor—I don't, usually, but that's the word chefs use on TV. Cheese, delicious light pastry, plus the bite of cayenne and a strong salty note of...

Fish?

The round tip of his nose twitched. "I await your judgment."

Since I'd volunteered as a tester, I owed him honesty. "What the hell is that fishy stuff?"

"I told you people wouldn't like it," Tory advised her father.

"Speak for yourself." To me, he said, "Anchovies."

"Dare I suggest it's an acquired taste?" That was the kindest critique I could offer.

His shoulders sagged.

"I'm sure it improves on acquaintance." Being fond of my roly-poly father-in-law, I finished the thing. Also, I was starving.

Tory folded her arms. "Back to you and Keith. What did you learn about Dr. Abrams?"

Carrying a glass of water to the table along with my second *gougère*—he was right; they weren't bad, once you got used to them—I devoted myself to my sandwich while weighing how much to share with my sister-in-law. Tory and I had joined forces previously on a couple of murder investigations that involved my patients, but only after she'd been hired by relatives of the deceased.

"Do you have a professional connection to the case?" I asked.

Impatience flickered across her deceptively sweet face. "Sort of."

I chewed my next mouthful at a deliberate pace. Normally, I dispose of my meals in a few gulps, having discovered as a medical student that I might be summoned away without warning. "Sort of how?"

After an annoyed huff, Tory clarified, "I checked out the nurse, Brandy Cornello, online. She posted that she's determined to get to the bottom of what happened to her doctor. I messaged her outlining my expertise and discretion."

Her father, transferring pastries to a platter, offered me another. I accepted. Anchovies are a good source of calcium and vitamins.

"And you believe that will inspire her to hire you?" I prodded.

"I may have alluded to my link to the medical community." She hunched defensively. Did she expect me to throw food at her? I'd hate having to explain fish smudges to my surly housekeeper.

I decided to stop being evasive, as far as my responsibility to Jeremiah allowed. "Keith interviewed one of my colleagues, who asked me to sit in."

"Why? What did he or she have to do with Dr. Abrams?" Tory demanded.

"He'd seen her Saturday night. Nothing obviously relevant to her death," I said. "Keith did bring up that OnWard and UpWard doctor, Radman. I heard him on the radio on my drive home."

"Anything worth sharing?"

"Her car was found outside his house," I said. "Also, he claimed Alison—Dr. Abrams—appeared at his door Sunday night, upset and rambling."

"Did he sexually assault her?" Tory asked.

I nearly choked on my sandwich. "Why would he confess that on the air?"

"I meant, have you heard of anything like that happening previously?"

"No." When Jeremiah brought up Alison's dislike of her former mentor, Keith *had* raised the possibility of a sexual offense. But if there'd been an earlier attack, why on earth had she gone to Radman's house alone on Sunday? "Have you?"

"Not in Safe Harbor," Tory conceded. "Still..."

"Still what?"

"There was an interesting case here about three years ago, while I was working crimes against property," she said.

"Rape isn't a crime against property," her father remarked from where he stood loading the dishwasher. "Except maybe in a few extremely backward countries."

"Good point, Dad." Tory resumed her tale. "We arrested a young woman for spray-painting 'rapist' on Dr. Radman's front wall."

I'd heard nothing of that incident. "Did she report a rape to the police?"

Tory shook her head. "No. She contended he'd raped her sister several years earlier in another jurisdiction. Azalea Springs."

That was the town where Radman had once mentored Alison. "What was her name?" I asked. "The woman you arrested."

"Katerina, goes by Kit. Last name Lopez. No, Sanchez."

"Doesn't ring a bell," I said.

"She was convicted of a misdemeanor and had to pay to remove the graffiti," Tory said. "Damn hard to get red paint off that stone facing, I imagine. Dr. Radman termed her mentally unstable."

I'd be mentally unstable, too, if someone had raped my sister. However, that neither proved nor disproved the accusation. "Did she harass him again?"

"Not while I was on the force," my sister-in-law said. "Anything else from Keith's interview?"

"Nothing I can share."

Her lip curled. Too bad for her. Jeremiah's situation was private.

Then it hit me that he *had* brought up something that concerned her, although not about the murder. "By the way, did Lydia ever tell you she consulted Dr. Abrams?"

"For what?"

"A checkup. A problem. Anything."

My father-in-law, who'd displayed only a casual interest in the conversation while cleaning up, paused with a plastic container in hand. He appeared riveted by the discussion of his stepdaughter, whom he'd raised from the age of three and had loved as deeply as his birth children, Tory and her brother, Barry.

"No. Wait!" Tory stared up, as if deciphering a code on the ceiling. "She once asked which doctor I saw, and I said that depended on my insurance. She was looking for an ob-gyn, preferably female, who didn't work in your building."

There were several excellent women ob-gyns at Safe Harbor Medical. What about Lydia's health had she been intent on safeguarding?

*Safeguarding from me.* That hurt. "Did she say anything else on the subject?"

"Later, that a friend recommended someone," Tory replied. "That was the last I heard of it."

"When was this?"

Another pause. "A few months before she died. Why, Eric?"

"I won't know till I get hold of her medical records." I tapped distractedly at my empty plate. "It didn't occur to me she might have had a health issue."

"What kind of health issue?" Tory asked. "Did she mention it to you, Dad?"

Shakily, Morris set the container beside the cooling pastries. "Not exactly. No."

We both stared at him. His evasiveness astonished me. Was it possible my normally straightforward father-in-law was keeping a secret?

"What is it, Dad?" Tory pressed.

"It reminds me of Nelle's death."

Tory and Lydia's mother had died in a single-car crash about fourteen years ago. She'd been drinking heavily. "I don't see the correlation," I said.

"Probably isn't one." Morris positioned pastries in the container. "Just a weird flash. She'd been seeing a doctor herself. For menopause, I think."

"You never told me that, Dad," Tory said.

"Why would I?" He waved a hand at the pastries. "These are hot. Put them in the fridge for me later, okay? I'm tired." He hurried around us and through the great room.

"Get those records ASAP," Tory commanded me.

"Don't worry. I intend to." Opening my laptop, I composed an email to Alison Abrams' office, requesting the release of my wife's records.

# CHAPTER FOUR

Forwarding medical data is a part of my practice in which I take little interest as long as my staff complies with the law, which allows up to thirty days to complete a request. As Lydia's executor, I was entitled to obtain her records within that period. As her husband, I wanted the damn things yesterday.

After sending my message to Alison's office with copies of documents confirming Lydia's death and my position as executor, I tried not to worry about when the results might arrive. Not only was this matter far from urgent to anyone except Tory and me, but her partner's staff must be overwhelmed with sorting out her responsibilities.

Over the next few days, rather than dwell on my impatience, I focused on the buzz about Alison. Local media outlined her background: a native of Chicago, she'd won a scholarship to California Southstate University, where she'd majored in biology. The key point of interest was that her adviser as an undergraduate had supported her admittance to the university's medical school.

That mentor, as Jeremiah had said, was Ward Radman.

A reporter for *The Safe Harbor Journal* harped on his connections to the case, including Alison's visit to him the night before her death and the discovery of her car near his house. On his Thursday evening radio show, Ward responded with offended dignity—or what passed for it—that he'd had nothing to do with Dr. Abrams' death and refused to tolerate libel by the press.

The threat of legal action had an impact. In the next morning's paper, a subdued follow-up focused on the high rate of suicides among physicians compared to people in other occupations. Was it the long hours and stress of the job? Excessive interference by insurance companies? Heavy med school debt, or easy access to drugs?

The article offered no answers.

At lunch, Jeremiah informed me of the latest scuttlebutt, that Alison's will left her half of the medical practice to her partner, her savings to her brother in Chicago, and her house to her nurse.

"You're listening to gossip now?" asked our tablemate, a wiry, sharp-tongued anesthesiologist name Rod Vintner. "That's new."

"It is not gossip if it is factual," Jeremiah responded. "I wish to learn the reason for her death."

"You're sure there is one?" asked our companion. "Maybe it was aliens or a poltergeist."

"That is not sensible. If the world is not sensible, life becomes chaos."

"A little chaos never hurt anybody." Rod chomped into his sandwich.

He was mistaken. But he didn't know about the disorder in Jeremiah's brain.

"If she was murdered, the will might indicate who stood to benefit," I said. "As in, suspects."

"You mean, aside from UpWard, OnWard, Loving-the-Sound-of-My-Own-Voice Radman?" Rod quipped.

"I have read that you should follow the money," Jeremiah said. "Therefore, the will could indeed be useful."

That raised several possibilities. "Aside from her brother, who's out of state, the beneficiaries are the nurse and Dr. Kane," I noted.

"You used to work with him, didn't you, Jer?" Rod recalled. "Any signs he's a homicidal maniac?"

Jeremiah blinked in surprise. "There were not. Chuck served in the military. In my observation, he is reliable and disciplined."

"And lethal," Rod said. "Don't those army doctors go to boot camp like everybody else?"

"I don't believe so." I'd read that physicians were required to take a leadership course rather than basic training.

The anesthesiologist shrugged. "Too bad. Firing guns would be the fun part. Say, I hear there's a betting pool about Alison's cause of death. Any idea who's running it?" Our scowls must have discouraged that idea, because he added quickly, "So I can avoid them."

"The coroner should release a preliminary cause of death within a few days." I'd learned that from previous cases. "Unless further tests are required."

"Could be a big pool by then," Rod said. "If one participated in such a tawdry activity."

Jeremiah considered. "I suspect you are employing sarcasm."

"You're improving." Rod didn't specify what he meant by that.

I excused myself to check on a patient in labor. She was progressing well but still hours from giving birth.

On my way out of Labor and Delivery, another doctor stopped me. Narrow face, sharp chin. For an instant, I couldn't place him and then felt like an idiot. This was Chuck Kane,

31

Alison's partner, in person.

"Eric?" he said. "I saw your records request. With the police searching the office and so on, we're a bit disorganized. I'm hiring a consultant to sort things out, but it might take a week or two. And then there's patient care. Know any ob-gyns interested in buying into a practice?"

"Not offhand. There are brokers for that sort of thing, aren't there?" I'd been fortunate that my father had invited me to work alongside him after my residency.

Chuck ran a hand through his thinning brown hair. Frazzled and tense, he had a pale complexion for a Southern Californian. "I guess I'll get around to that. Damn, I can't believe Alison's gone."

"I didn't know her well," I said. "But it's a terrible thing. Jeremiah's quite upset."

"Is he?" His forehead puckered. "I never did figure him out. Some of his patients complained about his coldness and others liked him. I wasn't sure how he'd handle a solo practice."

"He seems to have landed on his feet," I said.

Chuck glanced toward the doctors' lounge. "Man, I need coffee."

*I'd better hurry before he's off.* "Anything you can do to speed up my wife's file, I'd appreciate it." Should I mention that there were unanswered questions, doubts, fears? I settled for, "Did you ever meet Lydia?" Perhaps he recalled why she'd consulted an ob-gyn.

"Afraid not. I'll do my best." With that, Chuck hot-footed it toward the lounge, where the staff keeps a coffee pot filled.

A week or two before I got the records? Agonizing. But aside from burglarizing his office or hiring thugs to rough him up, there was nothing I could do to get the information sooner.

So I believed, until the following day.

Saturdays are a spillover for me. No regular appointments

and I only schedule urgent surgeries. However, another doctor, Paige Brennan, asked me to step in on several operations because her four-year-old daughter was sick, and two of my patients required emergency C-sections. It turned into a busy morning.

I'd been home less than half an hour when my cell rang. Not recognizing the number, I answered, "Eric Darcy."

"Excuse me for bothering you, doctor." The female voice had a soft burr. "My name is Brandy Cornello. I was Dr. Abrams' nurse."

Why was a central figure in the week's events, a woman I'd never met, contacting me? Perhaps she'd intended to reach Tory, who'd messaged her about investigating on her behalf. Except this was my number, not my sister-in-law's.

At the counter, I set down my plate of reheated leftovers. "What can I do for you, Miss Cornello?"

"I saw that you asked for your wife's records," she said. "While you're waiting for them, there are details I could fill in."

"You remember Lydia?"

"Quite clearly," she said.

Even if her memories proved routine, I was starving for facts. "I wasn't aware until this week that my wife had consulted Dr. Abrams."

A sharp intake of breath. "She didn't tell you?"

"Tell me what?"

Her pause was brief but significant. What the hell had Lydia kept secret? "Let's not have this discussion over the phone. The truth is, I'd like to ask a favor of my own."

I nearly said, "Fine. Out with it!" But I couldn't commit to cooperating without hearing more. "Yes?"

"The police just released Alison's house, and I'm afraid they missed important clues. I need someone to help me dig through it, preferably someone with medical knowledge." She rushed on. "They seem to think she killed herself. She didn't. She wouldn't. "

Poke through a dead woman's possessions? Under ordinary circumstances, I'd have declined. But Brandy was dangling an irresistible carrot in front of me. "Do you have the authority to do this?"

"Yes." A car horn bleated in the background. "I'm on my way there now. Alison named me executor and left me the house. The police already searched, and they listed what they took—her laptop, her phone, things like that. No suicide note, no drugs, nothing that implicates Ward Radman. He killed her, I'm certain of it."

Much as I craved insight, I had to be frank. "I have no training in crime scene investigation. You'd be better served by a professional."

"I don't want a hired gun!" she flared. "Dr. Schwartz, who used to be in our office, told me once that he admired you. If you'll help me go through everything, I'll share what I recall about Mrs. Darcy. You should hear this in person."

My resistance was crumbling. "If we uncover evidence, we have to turn it over to the police."

"Fine with me. Seriously! Please, Dr. Darcy."

I'd be meeting a complete stranger, a woman, in a house where another woman had been found dead. The list of what could go wrong stretched into the next county.

It was doubtful we'd stumble across anything the crime scene techs had overlooked. But what was it Brandy had expected Lydia to tell me?

I couldn't bear to wait another few weeks. Here was someone who not only knew what was in the records, but possibly more. Patients often speak freely in front of a nurse.

Brandy might be lying, manipulating, perhaps setting a trap of some kind. It was a risk worth taking.

"What's the address?" I asked, and wrote it down.

# CHAPTER FIVE

Alison's house lay in the inland part of Safe Harbor, in a neighborhood of straight streets and modest homes. Light blue with cream shutters, it had been built in the 1920s bungalow style, with a broad, covered porch. Flanking it, spiky orange-and-lavender bird-of-paradise blooms defied the overcast sky.

I parked behind a weather-beaten compact. Pacing the porch, a young African-American woman broke stride at my approach. Short dark curls framed a wide-cheeked face, with dark skin and tilted eyes. She'd worn jeans and a T-shirt for digging through belongings. It clued me, too late, that I should have changed from my slacks and shirt.

Having done a quick Internet search, I was able to identify her as exactly who she'd said she was. "Miss Cornello," I greeted her.

"Doctor." Rather than shake hands, she pivoted and unlocked the front door.

What an abrupt greeting. Under the circumstances, though, I saw no reason to take her prickliness personally.

Although the house had been recently occupied, musty air and the tenacious scent of long-ago cigarette smoke lingered inside. The curtains were old, the carpeting worn. Its scruffy appearance wasn't helped by an abundance of shoe prints, which I attributed to authorities.

This had been Alison's refuge, her personal space. If she'd chosen suicide, the crushing pain and depression must have overshadowed any concern that others would invade it. But if she'd been murdered, we were violating her all over again.

Or were we? She'd left her home to Brandy. This was her trusted friend, seeking justice. Surely that counted.

The front room extended the width of the house, divided by furnishings into a dining area with built-in cabinets and a living room stuffed with books and magazines, opened mail and assorted trinkets and gadgets. Framed photos of babies and mothers, presumably sent by grateful parents, hung unevenly on the walls.

"Is the whole house like this?" I dreaded the prospect of spending tedious hours sorting through junk.

"Alison loved being surrounded by her things." Brandy frowned. "Just follow my lead, okay?"

We had negotiated an exchange, I reflected. "How about we start by discussing my wife?"

"We'll get to that, I promise. I'd rather not hold that conversation on the fly." Whisking to the built-ins, she scanned the items on the surface. "See if there are any loose papers floating around the coffee table, okay?"

I resigned myself to a delay. "Can you be more specific?"

"Personal notes. Anything that involves Ward Radman."

As I complied, I recalled her declaration on the phone. "Why are you certain he killed her?"

"He's a fraud and a liar." Her voice resounded over the scrape of a drawer opening. "He claims she went to see him Sunday night because she craved his support. Crap! She told me she felt driven to confront him about issues from the past. Whatever turned her against him, it upset her so much she couldn't talk to me about it."

"You two were close?" *Stupid question, Eric. Alison left her the house.* But it was more a keep-talking remark than a real inquiry.

"When you're a black lesbian, you don't fit anywhere." Bitterness laced her words. "Your family refuses to accept you. Anything bad that happens, you must have brought it on yourself. At the clinic where I used to work, I had to keep my mouth shut. Women don't like the idea of a gay nurse. They don't object to a male doctor seeing them naked, but a lesbian? Alison was different. When I started assisting her four years ago, it was like coming home."

I lifted a crooked picture off the wall and checked for a hidden slip of paper. Nothing there, or behind any of the others. "Were you in love with her?"

From her hands, a stack of magazines dropped with a thud. "She was straight. Just kind and accepting."

Once we'd plowed through the living room, we moved to the kitchen. Boxes of cereal, a flowery metal cookie tin, a canister of coffee and numerous appliances barely left space on the counter to prepare a meal.

Warming to her subject, Brandy talked as we poked through the cabinets. "She encouraged me to be active. Meet friends, lovers, whatever. And stand up for my rights. The LGBTQ folks in Orange County are really supportive, or they were before a bunch of them splintered off into Ward's groups. Isn't that stupid?"

"I'm with you there."

"He's a bully." Brandy stood by the pantry holding a hand mixer as if she'd like to switch it on and shove it in his face. "But he's charismatic. When he came on the scene, I have to admit, I was kind of fan-girling, myself. Thrilled to death when he picked me to help organize a conference." Her voice grew shrill.

"Sounds personal." That brought to mind Tory's account of the woman who'd accused Radman of raping her sister. Choosing neutral words as best I could, I asked, "Did he behave inappropriately?"

Her head jerked, almost in a spasm. "This isn't about me. It's about Alison." Swinging around, Brandy slammed the mixer down so hard a beater fell off. I took that for a yes.

When the police had questioned her, I doubted she'd revealed this to them. Well, she had a right to withhold personal information not directly involved in the case. Besides, I'd come here to learn about my wife, not to scrape aside the ugly woodpile of Ward Radman's past and expose the squirmy truths underneath.

And yet...

More than ever, I wished Keith weren't so close-mouthed about investigations. What did he suspect? Had that bastard Radman drugged Alison, fatally overdosing her in the process?

All the more motive to search her possessions, for whatever Brandy believed had been missed.

We riffled through the bedroom—piles of clean towels and bedding atop the dresser, traces of fingerprint powder here and there—followed by the linen cabinet. Nothing of interest.

At the bathroom door, Brandy halted. "I can't go in."

"You discovered her body here. That must have been a shock."

"I'm a nurse. I've seen death before. But... I wasn't expecting..." Tears choked her.

"Stay here. I'll look."

I stepped past her into the narrow chamber. A tub and toilet occupied one side, a built-in counter the other.

Above the sink, a small cabinet stood open, emptied of whatever medications it had held. The shower curtain had vanished, if there'd been one. Muddy shoe prints on the tile might have been left by paramedics, whom I've been told usually arrive first and aren't fussy about preserving evidence. Understandable, since their job is to save lives.

The room had already been investigated—thoroughly, it appeared. Nevertheless, I said, "I'll check the drawers."

"Forget them. It wouldn't be here."

"What is `it'?"

"The evidence." With that vague reply, Brandy gestured toward a second bedroom.

It contained a desk and other office equipment, along with piles of medical journals. No computer; Brandy had mentioned the police took that.

"This is where we need to search," she said, as if we hadn't been doing that already. "You start there, okay?" She indicated a file cabinet.

"All right." While she poked through the desk, I assessed the three drawers, each with a label: Old Records, Reference, Personal.

Since I had no right to review patient information plus a complete lack of desire to squat on the floor, I passed on Old Records. When I tugged open the balky middle drawer, it overflowed with conference packets, medical studies and articles stuffed into files, many unlabeled. If Alison had had a system, it was clear only to her.

Brandy pointed. "Look in Personal."

I'd had enough. "You're her friend. You should sort through that."

"You're a doctor. I'd rather you did."

"Why?"

"Because you might recognize something."

As Alison's nurse, she was far more likely to spot anything of value. Furthermore, I was tired, dirty, and increasingly irritated. "Are you playing me?"

"What?" Brandy pursed her lips, which were dry and cracked. As, on reflection, were mine.

I dropped into Alison's desk chair—she'd been tall enough that it didn't cramp my legs—and dusted my slacks. "You promised to tell me about my wife. Get on with it."

She appeared to debate with herself before asking, "Then you'll go through the files?"

"If you insist."

She leaned against the door frame. "Mrs. Darcy requested a consult because she'd stopped taking birth-control pills for months and still wasn't pregnant."

I stopped breathing. Lydia had been trying to have a baby? After remembering to inhale, I said, "She never told me that."

Brandy folded her arms. "Women don't always confide in their husbands."

But we'd been best friends, partners. Not, apparently, to my wife.

*Quit wasting time on self-pity.* "The problem could have been me." Since I hadn't been aware she was ready for a child, let alone concerned about a delay, I hadn't had my sperm tested. "Was there a diagnosis?"

"Yes."

"What?"

"It's complicated."

To hell with that! "Uncomplicate it."

Brandy framed her answer cautiously. "She had a growth on her left ovary."

I got a horrible, sick feeling. "Cut to the chase, Brandy."

"Tests indicated it was probably cancer. Alison urged her to have a biopsy to confirm, but she postponed treatment. She did agree to be tested for a BRCA mutation. It was positive."

Mutations in either the BRCA1 or BRCA2 gene are

41

associated with a high rate of breast and ovarian cancer. Jewish women of Ashkenazi—Eastern European—descent are particularly at risk, as I advise women in my practice if there's a family history of such cancers.

While the mutation is far from a death sentence, ovarian cancer can be hard to detect in the early stages and has a nasty mortality rate. The signs are nonspecific: bloating, pelvic pain, a feeling of fullness. If Lydia had noticed symptoms, she'd kept them to herself.

That was no comfort. I'm a doctor. If I could have saved anyone, it should have been my wife. "Did she provide any reason for withholding this from me?"

Brandy stared down at her sandals, as if the crisscross banding fascinated her. My brain raced over hints I might have missed. It was like stumbling through a maze.

"Just that she needed to deal with this on her own," she said.

Springing up, I yanked open the top file drawer. Might as well get this over with while we talked. "If she had cancer, it was obvious she couldn't keep me in the dark forever." I could barely see the files through the mist in my eyes.

"We don't always think rationally, do we?" Brandy said.

"That's for damn sure." I'd tortured myself these past three years, wondering if my wife had loved me, if I'd misread and misunderstood her. "Was she angry with me? Resentful?"

"Respectful," Brandy said.

Odd choice of words. "In what way?"

"She spoke of you with, I don't know, deference. Like somebody she was afraid to disappoint."

I wasn't sure how to interpret that. Since the nurse offered nothing more, I threw myself into the task at hand.

Flipping through personal folders, I skimmed the name of a mortgage company, home repair services and warranties for major appliances. There were tax documents, as well as records from college and medical school.

In my agitated state, I had little hope of spotting a file that might hold a damning link to Alison's past. And then, so thin I nearly skimmed past, there it was.

# CHAPTER SIX

The thin file bore no label and contained only one document. When the sides parted beneath my fingers, a name on letterhead jumped out at me.

Azalea Springs Rape Counseling Center.

It was dated seven years ago. The letter contained nothing inflammatory, just an acknowledgement of a donation. If Alison had used it for tax purposes, however, why keep it in a separate file? Did it imply that she'd received their services?

I showed it to Brandy. "Is this the kind of thing you mean?"

Reaching out almost reverently, she stopped short of touching it. "Yes."

"Did Radman rape her?"

A quick, tight nod. "After drugging her. Years ago."

No wonder Alison had hated her former mentor. Had she really gone to confront him Sunday night? But why then, and why in private?

Speculation was fruitless. I needed facts, and for those, I turned to the nurse.

She confirmed that, according to Alison, the rape had occurred in Azalea Springs. But Alison hadn't reported it to the police, or shared it with anyone except Brandy. Why not? Because, afterward, Ward had insisted that by agreeing to have a drink with him at his place, Alison had been practically begging for sex.

She couldn't prove he'd drugged her. Worse, he'd threatened that, if she sought charges, he'd claim they'd been having an affair when he recommended her for admission to medical school and was now attempting to extort money from him.

How typical of a powerful rapist, to manipulate the victim. I didn't blame Alison for being afraid to go public. An arrogant liar can be more credible to authorities than a traumatized truth-teller.

In recent years, large enough numbers of victims had spoken out to force action against some prominent abusers. However, I suspected they'd barely scratched the surface.

"Did you tell the detectives?" I asked.

Brandy drew back. "No. Hearsay isn't proof."

"This letter isn't proof, either," I said. "Why did you insist on my help? You plainly believed we'd run across something like this."

She shrugged, as if her throat were too tight to squeeze out words. This went beyond her feelings about Alison, I thought. Far beyond.

"He raped you, too." When she stiffened, it was both a confirmation and a reproach. Since she remained silent, I went on surmising. "You assumed if you shared this with the police, they'd figure out what he did to you."

"It's none of their damn business."

Although I hated sticking a hot poker in an open wound, she'd chosen to involve me. "There has to be more you didn't tell the police. What is it?"

"Nothing."

"Does it have to do with why you believe Radman killed her?"

Her jaw thrust forward. "He has to pay."

"For the rapes? For her death?"

"All of it."

Since Ward had raped two or—including the sister of Tory's arrestee—three women, he'd doubtless violated more. According to what Keith has told me, sexual predators are frequently repeat offenders. Escaping punishment feeds their sense of invincibility. And who has more authority and more trust than a psychiatrist who positions himself as an advocate for the vulnerable?

"I have to hand this over to Detective Sparks," I said.

"I'm counting on it." Brandy's tension eased.

"You should do it yourself." Despite her understandable reservations, I believed it would be best for her to bring everything into the open.

"It has to be from you," she insisted. "No one will doubt *your* credibility."

"That's why you wanted me here?"

"When I told my family, they refused to believe Dr. Radman raped me." She struggled on. "They accused me of lying. My brother said it couldn't be true because I'm a lesbian."

Brandy *had* sought support. And the people who should have stood by her had dismissed her.

I'd always taken for granted the respect of my family and community. No doubt there were circumstances under which my word might not be accepted, but I'd never met with this type of contempt. If that happened, I wasn't sure how I'd react. With fury. Possibly lawyers.

After a glance at the remaining folders, I closed the drawer. "I'll swing by the police station."

"They won't like it, that you've been snooping," Brandy

warned.

Keith didn't like a lot of things I did. "They'll get over it," I said.

*

Although I'd visited the police station before, the two-story stucco building adjacent to City Hall loomed larger than in memory. Climbing the steps from the small plaza, I jumped when a siren blared behind the structure.

*Guilty as charged.* Guilty of what?

Alerted by my text, Keith lingered behind the desk in the lobby. When I entered, he surveyed me with the same expression I've seen him direct at a mug of flat beer.

Opening an interior door, he steered me to an interview room. In my naïveté, I'd expected to drop off the file and let Keith take it from there.

The room struck me as smaller and more claustrophobic than the one I'd viewed during an open house tour. The chairs on my side of the plain table were bolted to the floor. When Keith activated the recording device nested in a wall recess, red lights showed two video cameras positioned in opposite corners.

While stating our names, Keith donned gloves to scan the file. "Did anyone else handle this in your presence?"

"No."

He slid the file into an evidence bag. "Describe how you acquired this."

I reviewed the morning's events. Brandy's phone call, her insistence police had missed a clue, her appeal for my aid in searching. Our rummaging through Alison's house, and the discovery of this file.

Stone-faced, Keith prompted me with questions. Sitting across from my old friend reinforced my awareness that we were nearly twenty years out of high school. I noticed the

47

touches of gray and the sun-carved wrinkles, as no doubt he saw mine. We had become grown men, on different sides of a table.

He showed little reaction until I relayed Brandy's disclosure that Dr. Radman had raped both her and Alison, and that they'd never reported it. Keith leaned forward. "When and where did these rapes occur?"

"In Alison's case, in Azalea Springs. At least seven years ago, judging by the date on that letter."

"What about Ms. Cornello's?"

"I didn't ask."

"Were there drugs involved?"

"She indicated there were. No specifics."

However little Keith was sharing, the reference to drugs implied to me that these might have been a factor in Alison's death. But then, I'd already gathered that.

"Did Ms. Cornello say why Dr. Abrams went to see Dr. Radman Sunday night?" Keith asked.

"To confront him about the past." Noting the lift of his eyebrows, I added, "Doesn't make sense to me, either."

He blew out a frustrated breath. Well, the frustrated part was my assumption. "Maybe you should have asked better questions."

"You're right." Being a trained diagnostician didn't make me a criminal investigator.

My natural sympathy for a nurse who'd discovered her doctor's dead body had colored my reaction to Brandy. Attempting to view the situation from Keith's perspective. I had to admit she was a natural suspect, since she'd found the body and inherited the house. Opportunity plus motive. *If* this hadn't been suicide or an accident.

"Has the coroner released the cause of death?" I asked.

"It's pending." Not that he'd reveal it to me, anyway. Police and close relatives are entitled to that information; I was neither. "What I don't get, Dr. Darcy, is why you agreed to help Ms. Cornello. I wasn't aware you two were buddies."

"I'd never met her before," I said.

"Why did you go?" he growled.

Much as I disliked discussing a personal matter on the record, I saw no reason to be evasive. "Because it seems that Lydia was a patient of Dr. Abrams'. Nurse Cornello knew her. She promised to provide insights while I'm waiting for the medical records."

After a beat, he said, "Lydia, your late wife?"

"Yes. I wasn't aware until recently that she'd consulted Dr. Abrams."

Keith grew still. He'd known Lydia throughout high school and college, when she and I had dated. Not only had he been best man at our wedding, but he and Tory had broken the news of her death to me.

The Bureau of Consular Affairs in Israel, unaware that Lydia's sister was a member of the force, had requested that local police notify the family. Tory had collapsed when she heard, and Keith had held and comforted her, before driving with her to inform me.

"Did you learn anything else relevant to Dr. Abrams' death?" he asked.

"Not that I can think of."

He switched off the recording. "What did Ms. Cornello say about Lydia?"

Might as well share the whole business. "That she might have had ovarian cancer. And she delayed scheduling a biopsy to confirm it."

Keith stared at me. "You didn't know?"

"Lydia kept it secret." My lungs felt heavy. If he continued picking at this point, I might blow up at him.

His mouth worked, as if literally chewing over this discovery. "Why would she delay the biopsy? That's crazy. Maybe she didn't have cancer."

He was focusing on her medical choices, not her relationship to me. Good.

I cited Lydia's positive result on the BRCA test. "She may have been convinced she was doomed. Some women assume that."

"Was she?" he asked.

"Not necessarily." I explained that, by the age of seventy, about half of women with such a mutation will get breast cancer, compared to roughly seven percent in the general population. Thirty percent are likely to develop ovarian cancer, compared to less than one percent.

Keith paled beneath his tan. "Is Tory at risk?"

Oh, hell. In the shock of Brandy's revelation, it hadn't crossed my mind that my vibrant, crabby sister-in-law might be in danger. "She should be tested. If it was their mother who had the mutation, there's a fifty percent chance she'd inherit. Barry, too."

"Her brother could be affected?"

"Men can get breast cancer."

He accepted this without further discussion. "You'll warn them?"

"Of course."

We shook hands and I left, scolding myself. Keith had thought about Tory immediately. I should have, too.

I was descending the front steps when a woman's voice called, "Dr. Darcy!"

Damn. Caught off guard.

My instinct was to mutter "No comment" and walk away from the woman addressing me. Soraya Montenegro was beautiful, ambitious and annoyingly aggressive. In fairness, as a reporter, she had a job to do.

"Are you here about Alison Abrams?" She held up her phone, which I presumed was recording. "What's your connection to the case?"

Since I could hardly elbow her out of my path, I decided to see what I could learn. "Before I answer, you share what *you've* learned."

"Excuse me?" Standing on the Civic Center plaza, Soraya shifted the shoulder strap on her purse. A colorful outfit set off her milk-chocolate complexion: a feathered red hat above a navy-and-white suit, with red heels high enough to alarm a podiatrist. "I save my material for my stories."

"Then I'll save mine." I turned away.

"Hold on!" She halted me with a raised hand.

"Well?"

I could see her brain processing how to disclose the smallest amount necessary. "Okay. There's an item I just wrote up. Hasn't been released yet."

"What?" Forget being tactful. Since encountering Soraya previously, I'd filed her under Those-I-know-and-don't-love.

"A neighbor of Dr. Abrams' saw her car outside her house around midnight Sunday. But, after she died, it was parked near Dr. Radman's place."

"Interesting." This was news to me. But the neighbor might be mistaken. "What else?"

"That isn't enough?"

"Nope."

With a sniff, Soraya dredged up: "There's over an hour gap between the time when that nurse left Dr. Abrams' office to check on her and when she reported the body."

An hour. Long enough to search Alison's house, tamper with evidence, phone a third party for advice, or...? "Your conclusion?"

"She moved the car!" Soraya burst out. "Don't you think?"

"It's not up to me to speculate," I said. "That's it?"

Her eyes narrowed. "You have no intention of telling me anything, do you, doctor?"

There was honestly nothing I could reveal in good conscience. Certainly not the rapes. That information, for anyone other than the police, was both libelous against Radman and a betrayal of Brandy's trust.

"I might be able to clarify what you've learned." The press and the police aren't the only ones who know how to fish. "What was the cause of death?" While I couldn't be sure she'd teased this out, the coroner's office isn't exactly Fort Knox.

Across the street, a couple of cars swung into the community center. Saturday afternoons meant classes, club meetings and children's activities. In front of me, the reporter tapped her foot impatiently.

"It was asphyxia," she said. "She suffocated. Her stomach contents indicated the presence of a drug, but they haven't identified which one."

For the umpteenth time, I wondered where Soraya got her information. The woman must be more persuasive with other sources than with me.

"You offered to clarify," she went on. "Well, doctor, how could a drug suffocate someone?"

Since I rarely deal with overdoses, I'd have preferred to consult resources via my phone, but that would have body-slammed my leverage. "Suffocation means to die from a lack of oxygen." I scoured my memory. "Drugs can kill in a number of ways. They can drop blood pressure to dangerous levels, or cause cardiac arrhythmia, heart attacks and strokes. Or deprive the brain of oxygen, resulting in unconsciousness or death. Hence, suffocation."

"Could any of these drugs be legal?" she pressed.

"Something a doctor might have access to?"

"Certainly. For instance, we're having an epidemic of deaths from synthetic opioids." Those had been overprescribed for pain relief, resulting in widespread addiction.

"Dr. Darcy!" She glared at me. "The coroner didn't say she died of an overdose."

Fair enough. "For asphyxia, one prospect would be ketamine. It's an animal tranquilizer and was once used as a surgical anesthetic in humans."

The reporter nodded eagerly. I had hit on a topic she liked. "Isn't ketamine considered a date-rape drug?"

"I'm not crazy about that term, since the victim isn't necessarily dating or even acquainted with her assailant." In my practice, I had met victims of this odious crime. Often they weren't sure what had happened; they might blame themselves, especially if they'd been drinking. Naïve young women who think it's safe to party are easy targets for predators. "But yes. Ketamine has side effects that can appeal to a rapist. For example, it may produce a disassociative effect."

"English, doc." Soraya bounced with excitement. Or perhaps she was struggling for balance in those shoes.

A portly man in a suit, descending from the lobby, sucked in the sight of her, from those shapely legs on up. He glanced back twice as he headed for the sidewalk. *Out of your league, buddy.*

"A person feels like they're watching themselves," I told Soraya. "It's called depersonalization syndrome. Ketamine can also cause respiratory arrest."

"Meaning the victim can't breathe? As in, suffocates?"

"Yes."

"Does it have legitimate medical uses?" she asked. "For humans, I mean?"

"This isn't my area of expertise."

"You owe me!"

53

She could look up this information herself. But I supposed her article would play better if she quoted a source.

I recalled reading a study. "It has shown promise in treating post-traumatic stress disorder, PTSD. It allows the patient to review traumatic events without experiencing emotional distress."

Soraya's face lit up as if I'd offered her a foot massage. "Could a psychiatrist use it in his practice?"

"It's possible. Not common, as far as I'm aware." Much as I despised Ward Radman, I hadn't meant to smear him by implying a connection.

She tossed her head, then grabbed her hat to keep it from flying off. "If there *was* ketamine in her body, that's a major clue."

"It wouldn't indicate where she got it or how she ingested it."

"I suppose not." Soraya lowered her phone. "I'll expect more from you next time."

"Excuse me?"

"There's a price for everything, doc." Off she marched, unafraid of the very real danger of a twisted ankle.

That was two women I'd cheered up today, I mused as I reached my car. Brandy, by discovering the document from the counseling clinic, and Soraya, with the information about ketamine. Either revelation might land the obnoxious Ward Radman in well-deserved trouble, but I wouldn't count on it.

Now I had to go home and upset a woman I cared about. Not to mention how Morris might react to this news about his children's genetic heritage.

When I arrived, my father-in-law's catering truck was absent; in the late afternoon, he must be out distributing special-order meals. At the curb gleamed an unfamiliar, expensive convertible.

Since our cul-de-sac doesn't attract many visitors, I presumed Tory had a guest or a client. But what kind of client owned a sports car that cost in the hundred-thousand-dollar range and had a medical emblem on the license plate?

Hoping I was wrong about the visitor's identity, I drove into the garage.

# CHAPTER SEVEN

A serial predator. A pretentious loudmouth. Possibly a murderer. I hated seeing Ward Radman in my house. But there he stood in my kitchen while Tory poured two mugs of coffee at the counter.

Tall, with dark-blond hair unusually thick for a man in his early fifties, he had large owlish eyes and an insincere mouth. Also a gray cast to his complexion and wrinkles in his tailored suit. Feeling the pressure?

Tory was in no immediate danger from him. Point A, she was as tall as he was and in better shape. Point B, she held a cup of hot coffee and she knew how to use it. Point C, I was standing here, ready to spring to her defense, not that she'd have appreciated it. Point D, the jerk was presumably on the premises by invitation.

I hated that there were reasons *not* to punch him. There was even a Point E: surgeons don't get into fistfights and risk injuring their hands. Unless they're really, really ticked off.

After my conversation with Brandy, I was close.

"Oh, hey, Eric." My sister-in-law jerked her head in a butt-out manner.

I ignored her. This was *my* house.

56

"Ah, Dr. Darcy. We met when I spoke at the hospital." The psychiatrist brought the full force of his personality to bear on me: blinding smile, wide-open gaze, hand extended to shake.

And damn it, strictly from instinct, I shook it. He had a firm grip. The slime was metaphorical.

*I just spent a few hours with one of your rape victims.* The words stuck in my throat. A lifetime habit of civility can't be hacked up like a cat's hairball.

I had to admit, I was impressed at his memory. Or—*don't be naïve, Eric*—he'd researched Tory's situation and observed that her brother-in-law practiced at Safe Harbor. "What brings you here?" I asked.

"It's confidential." Tory's gold-flecked green eyes narrowed. "Let's go back to my office, Dr. Radman."

Ignoring her, he remained at the counter, tossing down his coffee. To me, he said, "My attorney hired Ms. Golden's services. He offered to liaise with her but I'm a hands-on kind of guy."

*In more ways than one.*

"As I mentioned when we signed the contract, I can promise discretion but nothing you tell me is privileged," Tory said. "That means I can be forced to disclose anything you say in court. That goes for Dr. Darcy, as well."

"I'm aware of what `privileged' means." His words had a dismissive edge.

Privilege, as Keith has complained to me, means that the law protects certain communications from being revealed in court. The most famous type is attorney-client privilege, but disclosures to a therapist are also included. Private investigators, not so much.

"Nothing I share with you is a secret. I'm hiring you to help clear my name, Ms. Golden, because I'm innocent." The volume increased as if Radman were addressing a large audience. "I'm glad Eric's here. Another physician's take on this situation could be valuable."

It must be my bonanza day for free consults. Still, I couldn't resist the temptation to listen to this creep attempt to justify himself. And pick up insights that might skewer him.

"More coffee?" Tory asked.

He set down his cup. "I'll let you know."

"My office, then. The two of us."

"I want Dr. Darcy present," Ward countered. "Seems like I'm being blamed for all kinds of things these days when I'm alone with a woman."

Unwilling to risk losing a client, Tory settled for leveling a warning stare at me. Fair enough.

Vowing to keep my thoughts to myself, I followed Ward and Tory through the great room and past the curving staircase. High overhead, the skylight filtered a pinkish glow that bathed pearl and aqua wall hangings, a memento of Lydia's decorating sensibility.

Tory's office occupied a former conservatory at the front of the house. Light flooded in through a bay window, partly screened by a dark-green camellia bush starred with rosy blooms. Inside, the only sign that this had served as my wife's art studio was a framed canvas layered with glass shards, photographic fragments and fabric scraps that coalesced into a portrait of a woman.

Behind the desk, Tory clicked on her recorder and ran through the same data Keith had used in interviewing Jeremiah: time, date, place and people present.

I settled in a chair. On his feet, Ward laid an arm across the top of a file cabinet, then snatched it away and brushed off his sleeve. My housekeeper would have been offended.

"Let's review your..." Tory didn't get a chance to finish her sentence.

"Someone is framing me." Radman thrust out his jaw. "And I can tell you who. It's that damn nurse, Cornello."

"She killed Alison to frame you?" I asked.

"I didn't say that."

"Start at the beginning, please." Tory's flat manner dared him, and me, to ignore or interrupt again.

"Yesterday, the cops searched my house, my car and my office." While this obviously wasn't the beginning, she let him continue. "I don't know how the hell they convinced a judge to issue a warrant. I did *not* put the baggie in the bureau. It was planted."

"The police found a plastic bag of drugs in your house?" Tory asked.

"They seemed to think that's what it was. It's being tested."

She considered. "Who had access to your house, besides you and Dr. Abrams?"

"My housekeeper. She's been with me for years. Someone could have sneaked in while she was cleaning, though." Radman began to pace. "At my office, the cops confiscated perfectly legal medications."

"What specifically?" Tory asked.

"Ketamine," he said.

I'd been on the right track with Soraya. "What do you use it for?"

"Treating PTSD. Some of my patients have been bullied and abused because they're gay or trans. You can't imagine what that's like." The volume rose. He'd begun speechifying again.

"What did you tell the police about the night Dr. Abrams died?" Tory prompted.

"That's the problem," he said. "Initially, I didn't give them the whole story. It was too sensitive."

I'll bet it had been.

"Initially? What about later?" Tory asked.

"After they retrieved that baggie, I had to change my story." He was twiddling his fingers.

"Did you happen to change it to the truth?" Tory asked.

"Of course!" Ward shook his head irritably.

"Which is?"

He commandeered the chair next to mine. "She rang my doorbell Sunday night, unexpectedly, and insisted we have sex."

"She insisted you sleep with her?" Tory's lip curled. She hadn't heard about Jeremiah's experience on the previous night, I realized, and wondered how the two incidents were connected.

The psychiatrist scowled at my sister-in-law. "See? You don't believe me. The cops didn't, either."

*Probably because you'd lied to them.*

"Did you have a prior sexual relationship with Dr. Abrams?" Tory asked.

"No. Yes. A long time ago." Ward waved dismissively.

"Did you have intercourse Sunday night?"

"We're two consenting adults," he retorted. "I used a condom. I was careful not to let any semen escape."

"Wise of you to take precautions," she observed tonelessly.

"I wasn't planning to kill her! I was concerned about pregnancy," he said. "As any sane man would be."

Tory resumed the narrative. "Okay, you had sexual relations. What happened next?"

"When I woke up, she was ..." He sucked in a breath. "Lying there, dead."

"Just like that?"

"Like what else?" Radman demanded.

"I mean, how could you be sure?"

"I'm a doctor," he snarled. "She had no pulse and she was cold. I performed CPR. It was hopeless."

"Did you call paramedics?"

"No." He tucked in his chin, puffing his jowls. "I panicked."

The damn fool. Assuming he hadn't killed her intentionally, he'd basically let her die. Paramedics can sometimes revive patients beyond the point where most people would consider them hopeless. At the very least, he should have dialed 911 so the coroner could be notified and the circumstances preserved.

"You panicked?" Tory repeated.

"You sound like the police!" Radman gripped the chair arms. "Okay, okay. I supposed that's why I hired you."

"What did you do once you concluded that Dr. Abrams was dead?"

"I felt foggy, like I'd drunk too much, only I hadn't. I must have been drugged."

She responded rapidly. "By her? Or someone else?"

"That's the damn thing!" he burst out. "It's crazy. You think I don't see that? If I'd been thinking straight, I'd have summoned help. But I've had people targeting me for years, seeking to destroy me because of my work in the LGBTQ community. I figured I'd been set up. I just wanted it to go away."

The guy was babbling. No sign of the glib, controlled personality I'd observed previously.

"Then what did you do?" Tory asked.

He'd driven Alison home in her car and placed her in the bathtub, Ward said, to hide trace evidence. He'd walked home—about two miles—and laundered his sheets, clothes, towels, whatever she might have touched.

"You admitted this to the police?" Tory prodded.

"Yes. After they discovered the baggie. Which was *not* mine."

She glanced at her notes. "You left Dr. Abrams' car parked at her house?"

"That's right," Ward snapped. "Someone moved it."

I recalled the hour gap between when Brandy went to check on Alison body and when she dialed 911. Also, if a neighbor really had seen the car at Alison's house late the same night, that would confirm Ward's account. The second one, not the lie he'd told police initially.

*It's much easier being honest. You don't keep mixing up your stories.*

"You suspect Dr. Abrams' nurse?" Tory asked.

Radman rolled his eyes. "Didn't you hear me? I was framed!"

My sister-in-law hung onto her temper. "Why would she do that?"

"A few years ago, while we were organizing a fundraiser, we had a brief hookup. She wanted more, and I wasn't interested."

While I preferred not to escalate this into an argument, I couldn't stay silent. "She slept with you voluntarily? Isn't she a lesbian?"

"Bisexual," he responded instantly. "And seriously messed up, which I should have noticed. After that, she started running me down to her friends, claiming I had no business representing a group I didn't belong to. As if commitment and expertise mean nothing. As if I hadn't raised sympathy for and awareness of their cause."

*And got a bestselling book out of it.* Plus a new crop of potential victims.

"How many women have you had sex with in the past three years?" Tory asked.

"I don't keep a tally!" Ward shoved back his chair. "That's enough. You can take it from here."

"Please bear with me, Dr. Radman," Tory said. "While this may be uncomfortable, the police will dig into your past, and your defense will need to know whatever they're likely to find."

His jaw twitched. "Okay, what else?"

The angle of her jaw told me the next question would be a tough one. And it was. "Dr. Radman, were any of your sex partners among your patients?"

"Never! That would violate medical ethics."

I believed him. Aware that sexual misconduct with patients could cost him his medical license, Ward had picked his victims carefully. He'd abused colleagues—a doctor he'd mentored, and one or more nurses—women who'd trusted him, and who'd been too shocked and confused and dubious of their power to retaliate.

My fists clenched. *Keep it together, Eric. This is Tory's show.*

"I'd like names and contact information for as many sex partners as you remember."

"Why?"

"We have to get ahead of the prosecution, if there is one. They'll be interviewing every..."

"I didn't kill Alison!" Ward huffed. "I'm a victim here. This whole experience has been traumatic. I've been suffering nightmares."

"About what?" I asked.

"Wouldn't you have nightmares if you awoke with a dead woman beside you?" he roared. "I refuse to go down for this! I've visited people in prison. It's claustrophobic. It's demeaning. Every time I hear a car stop on the street in front of my house, my heart pounds, like it's the police coming to arrest me. I didn't kill her!"

He wore the shocked, angry expression of a manipulator who's finally told the truth and no one believes him. That didn't mean he *was* telling the truth, of course.

As Tory bent over her notes, a reddish-brown cloud obscured her face. Every instinct in her body must be screaming that she'd love to see this jerk locked up. But she, too, had professional ethics, including an obligation to his attorney and to her boss at the detective agency.

Not that I agreed with her accepting the case. And I hated to imagine how Keith would react if—when—he learned she was assisting this worm. Not because everyone doesn't deserve a fair trial, but because it required her to spend time in this sleazebag's company.

"You don't have to convince me," Tory said. "I'm here to help prepare your defense, should you require one."

Her steadiness had a calming effect on Radman's fury. "Tell me how you plan to proceed."

"There are quite a few areas to investigate." She met his gaze. "Who moved Dr. Abrams' car, obviously. The police must have searched it by now. I'd like to know if they recovered the nurse's or anyone else's DNA. And there's the matter of that baggie."

"I'll bet it contained ketamine," Ward muttered. "It's no secret I keep some at my office."

"Medical grade?" Tory asked.

"Certainly!"

"The material in the baggie may not be identical," she said. "If it was bought on the street, it could contain adulterants. I'll check out the coroner's findings. and talk to the victim's colleagues and friends about her odd behavior, why she might suddenly show up seeking sex. There are a lot of loose ends. Whether or not they support your version of events, they can cast doubt on your guilt."

"That's not enough. I have to be exonerated, not get off on a technicality." The words rasped out. "I'm a psychiatrist and a public personality. My reputation is everything. That Cornello woman wants to destroy me."

Tory folded her hands on the desk. "Dr. Radman, I recommend you avoid hurling accusations at anyone, no matter how guilty you believe them to be. Take your cue from your attorney about how to conduct yourself. Avoid the press, and be straightforward with the police."

"They should be protecting me!" He was winding up again. "Once people start accusing you of wrongdoing, it turns into a witch hunt. I wouldn't put it past some maniac to try to take me out."

"Do you have reason to believe your life is in danger?" Tory inquired quietly.

"If it is, I'm ready to defend myself. I have a gun permit." Radman sprang up. "Psychiatrists deal with paranoid patients and I've always known something like this might happen. I'm a pretty damn good marksman, too. You're welcome to spread the word on that."

Tory arose as well. "I wouldn't publicize the fact that you own a gun. It could work against you."

"I'll do whatever I damn please!" He glared.

"I'm not the enemy," Tory reminded him. "It's my job to dig into the case on your behalf. I'd like to start by searching your house and car for whatever the police might have missed."

Despite a flare of the nostrils, he nodded. "Okay. What about Dr. Abrams' car?"

"I'll ask for permission to go over that, too," she said.

"The sooner, the better."

"How does tomorrow morning sound?"

They set an appointment for early Sunday. Just as I was wondering if I dared object to her being alone with Radman at his house, Tory said, "Okay if I bring another detective from my agency? We'll work faster that way. No extra charge."

"Fine."

When he left, I avoided shaking hands. Otherwise, I'd have had to soak my skin in bleach.

In the front hall, my sister-in-law faced me. "Just because he allowed you to sit in does *not* give you snooping privileges."

"I have zero desire to hang around with either of you tomorrow morning," I said. "Listen, there's another matter we need to discuss."

"Later. I want to write up my report while it's fresh in my mind." Off she went.

Cancer, genetics...a difficult conversation postponed. Just as well to leave it until after dinner. Before I reached the refrigerator, though, someone knocked on the door.

The return of Radman? I wasn't sure I could bear the sight of him again. Also, he'd struck me as more the bell-jabber type.

Hearing no response from Tory, I trudged to the front and opened up, hoping it wasn't Ward and that if it was, I could contain my disgust.

That proved unnecessary. It was a different doctor entirely.

# CHAPTER EIGHT

Judging by the bags under Chuck Kane's eyes and the stubble sprouting from his narrow jaw, Alison's medical partner had had a rough day.

"Hope I'm not disturbing anything." He stretched his shoulders. "Usually I take Saturdays off, but a couple of patients couldn't be postponed. I figured I'd stop by on my not-quite-way home."

"Good to see you." Puzzled, I opened the door wider.

"This isn't a social visit." He handed me a manila envelope. "My staff's overwhelmed right now and I'm hopeless with computers. Tried to email you the folder but—it was easier to print it out. I got your address from the file."

Lydia's medical records. My throat tightened. "I appreciate this."

Chuck stifled a yawn. "One more thing."

"What's that?"

"The coroner released Alison's body, and her brother, Andrew, is here from Chicago to arrange the funeral," he said. "He scheduled a graveside service tomorrow, 2 p.m. at Safe Harbor Memorial Garden."

"Thanks for telling me." I hate funerals. Too many losses in my life. Also, I hadn't known her well. "Did she have other family?"

"An elderly mother in Chicago, plus Andrew's wife and kids, but they're not flying out." Chuck didn't comment on this omission. "He asked me to invite a few close friends and staff. Dr. Schwartz is hosting a gathering afterwards at his apartment."

"Jeremiah is?" That startled me.

"There won't be a big crowd. We're only inviting a few people, to keep out the curious."

That meant my absence might leave too few mourners to honor her properly. "I'll be there."

We were shaking hands when Tory responded, belatedly, to see who was at the door. Courtesy required introductions, and her gaze sharpened at the discovery that Alison's partner stood in front of her.

"Dr. Kane, you've talked to the police already, I presume?" Receiving a nod, she explained that she was a PI investigating the case, without specifying on whose behalf. "Could we speak privately?"

"I'm afraid I'm in a hurry. Besides, there's nothing more I care to say."

She plunged ahead. "I imagine they asked about Dr. Abrams' drug use."

"They did. I wasn't aware of any." He scratched an eyebrow. What is it about being dog-tired that causes people to itch? My brain dredged up the answer: dry skin.

"Alcohol?"

"She drank socially. Partied occasionally."

"Who did she party with?" Tory probed.

"She never mentioned anyone in particular," Chuck said. "She liked that tavern, the one that has theme nights, like Elvis and oldies."

"The Suncrest Saloon?"

"That's it. Sorry, I don't know more." To me, he added, "I apologize for putting you off yesterday. Until Brandy emailed me this afternoon, I didn't realize your wife's records contained such a shocker."

Tory frowned. "What do you mean?"

Damn. This wasn't the kind of news to blurt in front of a stranger. "I'll explain in a minute," I said.

"I have to head out." Chuck swung around.

The Golden Fine Foods Catering van halted in the driveway. Out popped Morris, clad in a white chef's hat, white jacket and black pants. "Hello, hello!" cried my father-in-law. "Glad there's company. I'm loaded with leftovers. You wouldn't believe how much they over-ordered for this Sweet Sixteen party."

"My dad's a caterer," Tory explained. "Join us for dinner?"

Chuck wore the expression of a man trapped in a nightmare where the escape hatch keeps shrinking the closer he approaches. "Sounds great but I'm late already. I have to pick up my nine-year-old daughter from my ex-wife." With a nod to Morris, he set off at a lope toward his car.

"What shocker?" Tory repeated to me.

"I'd appreciate some help here," Morris called.

"To be continued over dinner," I promised, and hurried to bring in the goodies.

*

"No way am I taking that test," Tory said.

Dismayed, I regarded her over the empty paper plates littering the kitchen table. Our consumption of mini pizzas, hot dogs in barbecue sauce, fruit chunks and dyed-purple deviled eggs had barely dented the leftovers. Morris had urged us to indulge, since he'd already stuffed the refrigerator. "A simple blood draw and you'll have the results in a week or so."

"I refuse to live in fear." My sister-in-law eyed a plate of sugar cookies. "Dad, you should donate this stuff to the memorial gathering tomorrow. I'll take it over for you."

"Good idea," Morris said.

Which would provide a solid reason for her to attend. I didn't object, even though she'd be snooping for Ward Radman.

Over dinner, I'd related the facts about Lydia's more-than-likely ovarian cancer and positive BRCA result. I'd also cited the risk to Tory and her brother.

Her refusal to be tested disturbed me. "Tory, if it's negative, that would be reassuring. And if it's positive, there are options."

"I don't care if I have this gene." She picked up two cookies, then a third. Living dangerously.

"Everybody has the gene," I said. "Or rather, genes. Normally, they protect against cancer. It's the mutation that's the problem."

"I'm only fifty percent related to Lydia. There's no breast or ovarian cancer on your side of the family, is there, Dad?" Tory asked.

Morris's puffy eyebrows performed a small dance as he weighed his response. "Not that I'm aware of."

"So my risk is minimal. What did my grandparents die of, anyway?"

"Bad habits." Since we were waiting for more, Morris elaborated. "Smoking and drinking. Mama had emphysema and Papa had liver disease. As for your mother..."

"Mom died in a car crash, not from cancer," Tory said. "Lydia must have inherited this from her father."

"You're in denial," I said. "Your life could be at stake."

She smacked the table. "Shove it, Eric. It's my choice."

"Have the test," Morris muttered.

"I beg your pardon?" His daughter regarded him with surprise. He rarely pressured her about anything.

"Just....do it."

I recalled him mentioning that Tory's mother had consulted a doctor for menopause-related problems. "What were you going to say about Nelle?"

His chin trembled. "It...it might have affected her, too."

Tory stopped eating mid-cookie. "What do you mean, Dad? If Mom had ovarian cancer, you'd have known."

"I did know."

A shadow sucked the light out of the room save for a halo around our table, from the overhead globe. "What?"

"The surgery and chemo didn't work," Morris said. "She insisted we keep you kids out of it."

"Why?" Shock had reduced my sister-in-law to monosyllables.

"She had this notion she was protecting her children," he said. "You were in college, Lydia had moved to Boston with Eric, and Barry had just graduated from high school. She swore me to silence."

"You're saying her crash was deliberate?" Tory burst out. "Like it didn't devastate us when she drove into a tree?"

"It was terrible for you kids." Morris folded his hands. "For Nelle most of all."

"For you, too," I said.

"I was okay."

Not in my opinion. He'd used her life insurance to pay bills—medical bills, I supposed—and slept on a cot in the back of Golden Fine Foods. Despite his protests that he preferred to be on site for early-morning food prep, his spirits had visibly drooped. After Lydia's death, worried about the impact of another loss, I'd persuaded him to move into my downstairs bedroom. The change had raised his spirits and, to my surprise, had comforted me, too.

"I didn't know her disease could be hereditary," he said. "If

I'd warned you and Lydia, maybe she'd have gotten checked sooner. She might still be alive." Tears traced his round cheeks.

I wished like hell he had. Or that I'd observed something amiss. Plenty of blame to spread around, and all useless.

At the sink, Tory washed and dried her hands. Then she picked up her sister's documents from the counter, where I'd set them after skimming the folder to confirm the basics.

"Neither of you caused Lydia's death," she said. "Let's see if we can figure out why she really went over that cliff."

"For the same reason your mother drove into a tree, I'm afraid," Morris said. "Because she preferred to choose how she died."

"This contains new information," Tory responded. "Let's not pollute it with old assumptions."

Assumptions were pretty much all we'd had until now. My wife's professed reason for traveling to Israel had been to get to the bottom of a family mystery. Her grandparents on her father's side had survived the Holocaust and reunited, only to die in Israel when Avram was young. He'd told Nelle vague stories about the circumstances. Perhaps he hadn't known the details.

Orphaned, Avram had grown up in a kibbutz. At eighteen, he'd emigrated to the United States, where he'd attended university and trained as an optometrist. Frequently depressed, he'd killed himself via carbon monoxide poisoning when Lydia was three.

Was probing his story really the reason for her final journey? She'd revised her will before the trip, specifying that she be buried in Israel should she die there. Maybe she'd planned to commit suicide. Why? Shutting me out, shutting out Tory and Morris, had been cruel.

After Keith and Tory informed me of her death, I'd sent them away. Wandering through the house, bewildered and stunned, I'd fallen down the stairs, broken my leg and sprained my shoulder.

Since I couldn't travel, Tory had flown to Israel alone to arrange the funeral. She'd questioned her sister's tour guide, who'd shared that Lydia had planned to meet an unknown person in Jerusalem. When Tory contacted the kibbutz where Avram grew up to learn more about him, either they'd had no information or they'd stonewalled her.

Lydia's fatal fall had occurred at Masada, a mountaintop fortress where, in 73 A.D., nearly a thousand Jewish men, women and children had died by choice rather than be enslaved by the Romans. The day my wife toured the site, the temperature had soared above 100 degrees Fahrenheit, and Israeli authorities had concluded she'd collapsed from heat exhaustion while standing dangerously near a cliff's edge.

Had it truly been an accident? Had it been because of her diagnosis? Or had the person she'd met in Jerusalem disclosed information that motivated her to jump?

The greatest mysteries aren't the unsolved crimes or the undersea wrecks that people spend their lives seeking. They're inside us and our loved ones, right here yet veiled: the fears, the doubts, the compulsions that drive us to do the unthinkable.

"This is interesting." Tory was studying a photocopied sheet.

I dragged myself from dark reflections. "Yes?"

" 'Patient delaying surgery. Plans travel to Israel to discuss family medical history with relatives,' " she read.

"She never mentioned relatives." Not to me. "Who were these people and how did she contact them?" Tory hadn't discovered any phone, email or other records.

She replaced the papers in the envelope. "If my sister could track down this person, so can I."

73

I decided not to question how she planned to proceed. I ran across a quote once, that laws are like sausages—it's better not to see them being made. The same might apply equally well to investigations.

# CHAPTER NINE

On Sunday morning, I awoke with a sense of dread. Yesterday's conversation with a reporter, nearly forgotten amid subsequent events, had revived as a dream in which I endlessly chased a silhouette, trying in vain to seize her notebook to prevent my name being smeared across the newspaper.

What had I said? How much had Soraya quoted, and had she taken it out of context?

Awakening in my king-size bed, I contemplated venting my anxieties on the treadmill in the adjacent exercise room. However, while that would have delayed my moment of truth with the morning paper, it's astonishing how keen my sense of smell becomes when I'm hungry.

Someone was cooking.

I threw on my dark-blue bathrobe and was halfway down the stairs before I caught the rumble of masculine voices. With pleasure, I registered that my brother-in-law had dropped in.

The youngest of three siblings, Barry Golden was the easiest to be around. In the kitchen, he and his father stood at the stove with their backs to me, both short and a little round-shouldered as they prepared omelets with fried potatoes.

I averted my gaze from the printed sections scattered across the table. Not ready to face that.

"Aha," Barry remarked over his shoulder. "Another victim."

"That smells like pepperoni."

"It is," Morris said. "Want some?"

"Sure." I had to ask: "Why are two Jewish guys fixing pepperoni omelets?"

"We had to remove the pork products from the food Tory's serving at the gathering this afternoon," Barry explained.

Leftovers for breakfast, hand-picked from other leftovers. Any self-respecting guy would decline. "Sounds great," I said. "Speaking of Tory, where is she?"

"Gone to that pervert's house." Morris cast a handful of grated cheese onto the egg spread, which he folded over.

Barry flipped hashed-brown potatoes with expertise he'd developed as a teenager, assisting at the catering company. Great hand-eye coordination. While I'd never observed him in the operating room, he had an excellent reputation as a urologist.

"Did she take someone with her?" I hoped so.

"Yes, that other woman from the agency," Morris said.

Good. Like Tory, Patty Denny was a former policewoman, in shape and no-nonsense. A guy who put a move on her would be missing a few teeth.

A couple of flourishes, a dollop of sour cream on the side, and Barry whipped a plate in front of me at the table. "Coffee, sir?" He quirked an eyebrow.

"Yes, and keep it coming. I tip well," I told him.

"Don't push your luck."

As usual, Tory had crumpled the paper. Today, her messiness was the least of my concerns.

*If you ignore it, maybe it'll disappear.* There's nothing like magical thinking to improve the flavor of breakfast, especially when accompanied by excellent coffee.

However, I had unpleasant news of my own to share. "Barry, I got hold of Lydia's medical records."

"Yes. I was sorry to hear she had cancer." He returned to the stove.

"Also, she tested positive for..."

"A BRCA mutation," he finished, filling his own plate. "Tory and Dad spilled the whole mess to me already. I'll get tested."

Simple and straightforward. That's my brother-in-law. "Great."

At the table, Barry opened the comics, leaving me the front page. Grimly, I straightened it.

"Stories Conflict in Doctor Death Probe," read the headline. Mercifully, it didn't add, "M.D. Shoots His Mouth Off."

In fact, I was cheered to discover, Soraya's story didn't mention me at all. Instead, it put Brandy on the hot seat.

"Questioned about the hour gap between when she left the medical office to check on Dr. Abrams, and when she summoned authorities, Cornello attributed the delay to her lack of a key. She told this newspaper that she knocked and rang the doorbell, then circled the house peering in windows."

Arousing no response, she'd searched for a hidden key, according to the story. Once she entered the house, the gruesome discovery of the doctor's body had shaken her so badly, it had been several minutes before she dialed 911.

Soraya quoted a neighbor who swore she'd seen Alison's car outside her house very late on Sunday. The story noted that its ultimate location in front of Dr. Ward Radman's home lay only a few miles away, a distance from which a person could speed walk to Dr. Abrams' house in under an hour.

Brandy denied moving the car.

Next, citing an unnamed source at the coroner's office, Soraya indicated the preliminary cause of death was suffocation, pending results of further testing. There was no reference to a suspicious substance recovered from Ward's house and no speculation about ketamine. I wondered if that was due to the intervention of the newspaper's lawyer.

The rest of the piece provided background on Ward. I skimmed the references to his bestselling book and radio show, his prominence as a supporter of LGBTQ rights, his medical training and specialty in psychiatry, and his part-time position on the faculty at California Southstate University.

The personal stuff interested me more. He had been married twice. Apparently his divorce had stirred a nasty court battle amid accusations that he'd dumped his wife for a graduate student, which must have been true, since he'd promptly married her. The second Mrs. Radman had died a few years later in a single-car crash with her husband at the wheel.

He'd told police they'd been arguing and she'd grabbed the wheel. When he overcorrected, the car flipped, rolled and burst into flames. His wife hadn't been wearing a seatbelt. He had, and escaped with minor injuries.

The incident had occurred late at night, on an isolated road. No drugs or alcohol were involved, and no charges had been filed.

While there was nothing concrete, the implication was that Radman had a history of disposing of inconvenient women.

Barry chuckled at a comic strip. Despite having been informed that he was at risk for a deadly genetic mutation, he continued to live in the moment. Being around him was good for me.

Having dodged a blow, I enjoyed the rest of the paper. Now all I had to survive today was a funeral.

*

Although the forecast didn't include rain, clouds dominated the sky when I parked at Safe Harbor Memorial Garden.

Crossing the lawn, I saw a plain wooden coffin in position to be lowered into the grave. A microphone, a large spray of flowers and a dozen chairs—mostly occupied—had been set up.

I signed the guest book on a portable table and took a folded program. It bore a smiling photo of Alison, details of the ceremony and information about the post-event gathering.

Jeremiah, wearing a gray suit and a blue yarmulke, reached into a basket and handed me a skullcap. "Hello, Eric."

I accepted the knitted round hesitantly. "Is it okay for me to wear this? I'm not Jewish."

"Yes, it is fine."

As I fitted it atop my head, I didn't ask why he'd been assigned the task of handing out ceremonial headgear. Judging by the modest attendance, there was a shortage of Jewish people present to fulfill such tasks.

I recalled that, according to Chuck, they'd deliberately kept the service private. While a public announcement would have allowed patients and colleagues to pay respects, the manner of Alison's death had generated a lot of publicity. I was glad we didn't have to deal with nosy intruders or members of the press.

I'd spotted one of those in the parking area. Soraya Montenegro had been arguing with Keith, whose scowl dissuaded me from greeting him. The reporter had a lot of nerve showing up here. Also, she was distracting the detective from his purpose, which was no doubt to watch who attended and assess their attitudes.

Approaching the chairs, I exchanged nods with Chuck and Brandy. Flanking them were several women I presumed to be office staff or close friends. If anyone had mentioned the event to Ward Radman, he'd had the sense not to put in an appearance.

By the casket lingered three men in suits. "That is her

brother, Andrew." Jeremiah, who had followed me to the seats, indicated a fellow wearing square glasses.

Andrew Abrams wouldn't stand out in a crowd: middling height, on the thin side, with light-brown hair. He wore a black ribbon and a green skullcap, and spoke quietly with a man in a white, fringed shawl.

"That is Rabbi Mainz," Jeremiah said.

Lydia had never mentioned a Rabbi Mainz. But then, I didn't recall her attending services except for special events. Neither did Morris or Tory, although they occasionally lit candles and said a prayer on Friday nights.

The third man, who I guessed worked for the funeral home, nodded to the rabbi. At this cue, the rabbi stepped to the microphone and recited a prayer in what I presumed to be Hebrew. He repeated in English: "The Lord is my shepherd; I shall not want..." Even a religious blockhead like me could identify the Twenty-Third Psalm.

Continuing in English, the rabbi welcomed us to this ceremony in memory of Alison Abrams, beloved sister, daughter and physician. More prayers followed, in both languages, after which he requested that we pray silently.

Beside me, Jeremiah's lips began moving. I couldn't hear what he said—*that's the definition of `silent,' Eric*—but I gathered he was repeating a familiar text. I wished I knew what to ask for. Guidance, I supposed.

How about, *God, please help me figure out what the hell to do next.*

The rabbi's soothing voice terminated my mental dithering. "Alison's brother, Dr. Andrew Abrams, will deliver the *hespeid*, or eulogy."

"He's a doctor?" I murmured to Jeremiah.

"Clinical geneticist."

This man diagnosed genetic abnormalities and counseled

people at risk, like Tory with the BRCA mutation. Not many years ago, our genes were a complete mystery. Now we have specialists.

At the mic, Andrew adjusted his glasses and consulted his notes. When he lifted his face, he regarded us as if worried we might whip out machine guns and mow him down. To his credit, he didn't let that stop him.

"In Jewish tradition, one of the most significant *mitzvot*—commandments—is to help our loved ones to their final rest." He cleared his throat. "The best way for me to do that is to tell the truth about Alison. The whole truth, not the pretty one."

I questioned the merits of this I-come-to-bury-Caesar-not-to-praise-him approach. But I was not the one speaking for the dead today.

"Although my big sister encountered more than her share of difficulties, she hid her troubles," Andrew said. "She was a brilliant student, and devoted her life to helping people. I wish she had cared more about helping herself."

He gazed past us, as if Alison stood listening. Maybe she *was* there, strong face tilted, hands on hips. I pictured her frowning, as she usually did in Labor and Delivery, except when preparing to walk into a patient's room. Her manner would change, a reassuring ray of golden light replacing the sepia tone.

"Our dad ran out on us when I was seven and she was ten," he said. "Our mom did her best, but she's hard to please, and she was hardest on Alison. My sister struggled to be perfect.

"I regret not standing up for her," Andrew went on. "The fact is, I was too immature to grasp what was happening."

He removed his glasses and wiped them with a small cloth. After restoring them, he said, "She played soccer in high school and was damn good at it. Until senior year. Suddenly she dropped the sport. Our mother called her a quitter and

81

complained she would lose her chance at a scholarship."

Why dwell on this incident at the expense of their mother? But at such an emotional time, a brother could be forgiven for wandering off course.

"Instead, she landed a scholarship to California Southstate University based on academics," Andrew said. "Several years later, her soccer coach was arrested and convicted of molesting a couple of girls. Was Alison a victim? Was that why she stopped playing soccer?

"If so, I wish she'd spoken up," he said. "Whatever happened, I believe it affected everything she did, including her choice of career. She picked a specialty in which she worked almost exclusively with women. And she avoided relationships. I assumed that, eventually, she'd meet the right guy, someone to love her. Someone she could trust. Too bad she never did."

*Someone she could trust.* She'd relied on her mentor, Ward Radman. According to Brandy, he'd repaid that trust by raping her. Had he murdered her, too?

A chill that had nothing to do with the cool weather penetrated my bones. In the next row, tears ran down Brandy's face.

"We may never learn for sure how or why she died," Andrew went on. "Did she kill herself with a drug overdose, as some have speculated? In the past, Judaism considered suicide a sin. Today, many of us view it as death by a disease, a mental disorder called depression. Maybe, if I'd had the courage to love her more, her life might not have been left unfinished."

He choked to a halt. The rabbi watched him closely, ready to step in.

*Unfinished.* The word echoed in my head, reminding me of Lydia.

Two women were dead, women whose lives had intersected. Although they'd died halfway around the globe from each other and several years apart, to me, their fates seemed linked.

Andrew had cited a commandment to help our loved ones to their rest. It might have been egotism but, at that moment, I felt compelled to seek answers for Lydia and for Alison, not to rely on the police or anyone else. Perhaps God had heard my plea for guidance and had handed me—or I had handed myself—a mission.

At the front, Andrew regained his composure. "In my sister's memory, I will hold my children closer. I will communicate with my wife more honestly. I will stay in touch with my patients. I will imagine Alison's spirit is with me in everything I do, as a doctor and as a human being."

He handed the mic to the rabbi, who read another prayer in Hebrew. When he finished, the funeral official released a mechanism that slowly lowered the coffin. Very smooth, very dignified.

"In Jewish tradition, placing earth in the grave of a loved one is an important act of love and service," Rabbi Mainz concluded. "Participation is voluntary. I will begin by sprinkling earth that has been brought from *eretz* Israel, the land of Israel."

He tossed in a handful of soil, as did Andrew. I followed Jeremiah to the grave, where we and the other mourners added contributions from a small mound. The funeral director provided hand wipes.

After expressing condolences to Andrew, Jeremiah and I set out for the parking area. "Will you attend the gathering at my apartment, Eric?" he asked.

"Yes. Fine," I responded automatically.

"Are you annoyed with me?"

"What?" I regarded my bony companion in surprise. "No."

"You do not usually respond in such a sharp fashion unless

you are annoyed," he observed.

I hadn't known he was aware of what, until this week, had been my customary reaction to him. Evidently, his inability to read moods had exceptions. "It's not you. Some of what Andrew said bothered me. I'm struggling with my reaction."

Jeremiah halted near his car. "I did not believe you wrestled with emotions."

How had he reached that conclusion? I had collapsed and fallen down the stairs in my grief over Lydia's death. But of course he hadn't seen that. "Sorry to disappoint."

"I am not disappointed." Jeremiah unlocked his car. "Now I must hurry to greet my guests."

As he pulled out, I waited for other cars to roll past. That's why I didn't hear the footsteps until Keith said, "Looks good on you." He indicated my head.

I reached up and removed the yarmulke. "Oh. I'll return it to Jeremiah at the get-together."

"Will Tory be there?" he asked.

"She's bringing food, yes."

"You talked to her about that test? The genetic thing?"

He didn't normally comment on other people's health issues. Tory meant a lot to him, despite their breakup. "She declined. She's being stubborn."

"Being stupid," he muttered.

"I'd avoid insulting her to her face, if I were you."

"Duly noted." He pivoted to leave.

A black sports car with white racing stripes nipped past. The rabbi was at the wheel.

Keith pivoted toward me. "I heard Tory's been inquiring about Radman. Please tell me she's not working for him."

"Wish I could."

"Damn!" He strode off.

A ray of afternoon sunlight on my face reminded me that it

was Sunday, a rare free day, and tempted me to escape to my den. To retreat with my unsettled thoughts and unsettling regrets.

*"One of the most significant commandments is to help our loved ones to their final rest."* Less than half an hour into my mission, I was already considering blowing it off. If there were insights to be gained about Alison, the place to start would be at Jeremiah's.

In my car, I entered his address into the computer. The directions took me across Safe Harbor to a neighborhood of one-story houses and duplexes, where I wedged into a space at the curb.

Alongside a ranch-style home, a driveway led to a freestanding double garage topped by an apartment. Above a steep staircase, the door stood open.

A couple of women I'd seen at the funeral paced ahead of me. When I slowed to prevent awkwardness at the stairs, a flutter of curtains in the house drew my attention.

An elderly woman with frizzy pink hair peered out the window. This must be the infamous landlady.

Behind her, someone shifted into view. A dark, attractive woman wearing a canary-eating grin.

Soraya Montenegro was getting her story. And it would be at Jeremiah's expense.

I hurried up the stairs, debating whether warning him was more likely to help or harm.

# CHAPTER TEN

It didn't take many people to fill the living room of the small apartment. A large, sagging sofa and a couple of chairs were occupied by guests with paper plates in their laps, while others clustered around Andrew and Jeremiah. I had to edge past them sideways.

Since I judged it inappropriate to shout an alert to our host, I scanned for—and spotted—Keith. He was lounging at the kitchenette counter, where Tory stopped refilling a pitcher of iced tea to glare at me. My guess: Keith had been haranguing her about working for Radman, and she blamed me for telling him.

"Hey." I addressed him, ignoring her. "Our unfavorite reporter is in the house, grilling Mrs. Linden."

"No grilling required," he answered. "I'm sure she's happy to spill."

That meant the entire world would soon hear the details of Jeremiah's night visitor. That might lead to confrontations, speculations, and revelations. "Can't you stop her?"

"Afraid not." Keith scooped up a handful of sweetened popcorn. "Did you know there are candy eyeballs in this?"

"Sweet Sixteen party," Tory said.

I set down my overlooked yarmulke. A scan of the trays on the counter revealed pink and purple cupcakes, sugar cookies, purple deviled eggs, little hot dogs in barbecue sauce and mini pizzas. Anchovies had replaced the pepperoni.

I couldn't blurt my concerns about Jeremiah in front of Tory. While I wasn't sure how much she knew about my colleague, as long as she worked for Radman, she had to remain out of the loop.

"How could you *not* have known?" Brandy's shrill comment pierced the hum around us. "My God, your sister was molested and your family abandoned her!"

Her accusation shocked the gathering into silence. Perhaps alone among those present, I understood that the real source of her fury was her own experience. When Brandy had summoned the courage to reveal that she'd been raped, her family had dismissed it. She carried a lot of anger, justifiably, but had chosen an unfortunate target on whom to unload it.

Chuck placed his glass of iced tea on an end table, preparing to intercede. Brandy was, after all, his employee.

Before he could act, Andrew spoke. "I share your outrage. But please bear in mind that I was a high school student."

"And a boy," Brandy hurled.

"Remember where you are," Chuck muttered.

Two women arose from the couch, leaving their plates on the coffee table. "We've got this, Dr. Kane," the older one said.

"Brandy?" The younger woman touched her arm. "Why don't we go for a walk?"

Judging by the nurse's rigid stance, she might have refused. Then her plastic cup tipped, spilling tea onto the worn carpet. "Oh! Dr. Schwartz, I'm sorry."

"It is fine," Jeremiah assured her. "I have purchased a spot remover recommended by the store clerk."

His earnest statement brought a smile. "That should do the

trick. Sorry for creating a scene." Head lowered, Brandy left with the two women. A couple of others slipped into the vacated seats.

Too bad Jeremiah hadn't escorted them. I could have seized the chance to warn him about Soraya while there might be time to intervene.

"I apologize for Brandy," Chuck told Andrew. "She was your sister's nurse."

"She's the one who discovered Alison's body?" He pushed his glasses higher on his nose. "No wonder she's distraught."

Since we hadn't been formally introduced, I thrust out my hand. "I'm Eric Darcy. I knew Alison professionally, and my late wife was her patient."

"Eric's an ob-gyn." Chuck went on to identify the remaining handful of guests, most of whom worked in his office. "You've met Detective Sparks. Ms. Golden, who kindly provided the refreshments, is a private investigator."

Amid the flurry of greetings, I tried to catch Jeremiah's eye. Until recently, he'd watched me closely whenever we were in proximity. Today, he focused on Andrew.

I understood his interest when Jeremiah said, "Dr. Abrams, I understand you are a geneticist. My grandfather was a Holocaust survivor and I have read that that might predispose my family to mental illness. Is this correct?"

Andrew responded thoughtfully. "Studies of children and grandchildren of Holocaust survivors do show an increased vulnerability to depression and PTSD."

"From the environment in which they're raised, right?" Chuck asked.

"That's what psychologists used to believe. However, recent studies indicate there's an inherited susceptibility," Alison's brother replied.

"People's DNA doesn't change in a single generation," Tory

blurted from behind the counter.

"That's correct." Andrew's composure reminded me that he was accustomed to dealing with patients' negative reactions. You must get a lot of those when you tell people their genes are playing cruel tricks on them or their children. "The change occurs not in the genome but in the epigenome."

"The what?" Keith was, as usual, impatient with unfamiliar terms.

"Picture the epigenome as a group of chemical on-off switches," Andrew said. "They modify how genes function, activating or deactivating them. Changes in epigenetics can occur in a single generation, and may be inherited."

"And that could affect Dr. Schwartz's family?" a woman asked from the sofa.

The geneticist nodded. "Descendants of Holocaust survivors often show altered levels of stress hormones compared to Jews the same age but without that background."

These studies might have implications for my patients, as well. "Would this apply when the mothers have been subjected to other types of trauma?"

"Most likely," Andrew said. "Fathers, as well. While it's hard to track individual cases, we see the effect on large groups, such as Cambodian refugees who suffered under the Khmer Rouge in the late 1970s."

"You mentioned depression and PTSD," Jeremiah said. "What about schizophrenia?"

I tensed, concerned about how much he might reveal. No one else appeared to react.

"That's a bit more complex." In social settings, doctors dislike being asked for a drive-by diagnosis, but Andrew seemed at ease expounding on this topic. "The reports I've read haven't identified an increased risk of schizophrenia in Holocaust descendants, but in those who do suffer it, there's often an elevated severity."

"They get sicker," Jeremiah clarified.

"Precisely."

There were no further questions. In the ensuing conversational lull, Andrew wandered to the counter for a refill of iced tea. Jeremiah peered out the window.

"What do you make of that?" he asked me.

"That" was Soraya, teetering in the driveway on her high heels while the pink-haired landlady jabbered at her. The reporter was edging toward the street. Apparently, Mrs. Linden had already gossiped more than enough to fill a news article.

Whatever the damage, it had been done. "I think we should leave unwell enough alone."

"Mrs. Linden is not always accurate. It is my obligation to set the record straight." With a pardon-me to his guests, Jeremiah ducked out the door.

After years of taking my advice, why did he choose this moment to ignore it? Well, that might be healthy, I mused as I went after him down the stairs.

"Dr. Schwartz!" Soraya swung toward him, dark eyes alight. "I've heard very interesting things and would love to get your side of the story."

Mrs. Linden folded her arms as if defying him to contradict her tale. Tory and Keith, who'd trailed me, halted within earshot. Frustrated, I could only hope Jeremiah wouldn't mention his schizophrenia.

Soraya held up her phone, capturing him on video. "According to your landlady, Alison Abrams spent several hours with you in your apartment Saturday night. Is that true, Dr. Schwartz?"

"Indeed." Jeremiah eased back, maintaining his personal space. In my opinion, while being videoed, the appropriate distance would be about half a mile.

"What were you and Alison Abrams doing?" she asked.

*Please don't...*

"We had intercourse," Jeremiah said. "At her request."

Tory jotted notes. This ought to help her client, I thought irritably.

Soraya beamed up at Jeremiah. "Why would she do that? Had you been intimate before?"

"No. I did not question her motives."

"Did she seem confused or under the influence?"

"Not at all," he said.

"Dr. Ward Radman claims she arrived at his house the next night and had sex with him," Soraya continued. "Would you say her behavior fits a pattern?"

"I would not."

"But she did the same thing!"

"It was not the same," he replied sternly. "Alison and I had been on friendly terms. Toward Dr. Radman, she expressed animosity. It would not be sensible for her to seek intercourse with him."

The reporter practically levitated with glee. "You're accusing him of lying?"

"I have no opinion on that subject," Jeremiah said. "Your questions have been answered. I consider this interview concluded."

If so, he might escape without too much damage. But Soraya hadn't finished. "Why did Alison hate Ward Radman?"

"I did not say she hated him. Only that she had a profound dislike."

Good answer. Now he should retreat.

"Profound dislike. Strong animosity," Soraya repeated, savoring his words. "What kind of behavior on his part would arouse such loathing?"

Jeremiah's jaw tightened. "I do not care to speculate."

"Use your imagination," she said.

"I am more concerned that my imagination might use me. Or abuse me."

She braced her phone-holding hand, which had started to waver. "I beg your pardon?"

Didn't the man see the quicksand in front of him? "It's a figure of speech," I interjected. "Jeremiah, your guests must be wondering what's taking so long."

A tilt of the head indicated he understood. "Dr. Darcy is correct. I am a host," he told Soraya. "I trust you will quote me accurately."

"I'll quote you, all right." With a satisfied smile, she whisked down the driveway.

Mrs. Linden scowled. She'd lost what I guessed to be her best audience to date.

Jeremiah studied me ruefully. "I believe I should have heeded your advice to leave unwell enough alone, Eric."

"Let's go in." I indicated his front window, from which people were peering down.

Inside, despite Tory's offer of more refreshments, the gathering broke up minutes later. Keith stuck around while she stowed leftovers in Jeremiah's fridge.

After I shook hands with Andrew and took my leave, it occurred to me that I might never see him again. However, in my mind, the intensity of the occasion had linked our lives irrevocably.

His remarks about the Holocaust's long shadow offered new insight into my wife's moods. Speaking of genetics, Tory approached with an aggrieved expression. "Why did you tell Keith about the BRCA test?"

Oh, *that's* what had been bugging her. "It came up when he interviewed me about Nurse Cornello," I recalled. "She told me about it."

She scowled, mulled this disclosure for a nanosecond, and moved on to: "He's nagging me. If I don't want the test, that's my business."

Keith appeared at her elbow. "If you don't get it, you're an idiot."

A real diplomat, was my old friend.

"Why do you care?" Tory shot back.

"I don't want you to die." He shrugged. "Think how boring life would be."

"You *like* drama? That's a change."

To my surprise—and hers, I'm sure—he blinked, hard. Were those tears lurking? "Take the damn test."

She was so stubborn, I worried she might refuse out of spite. Instead, she asked me, "Care to recommend a doctor of the female persuasion?"

At this sign of acquiescence, Keith had the sense to refrain from comment.

Easy answer on my part. "Paige Brennan. She has an office in my building."

"I know her," Tory said. "Her husband's my boss, remember? He co-owns the detective agency."

"I hope that's a yes."

"Why not? Otherwise I'll never hear the end of it from you two."

Whether Keith had simply worn her down, or his show of emotion had had an impact, didn't matter. I was simply glad, considering what a bunch of scandalous suppositions Jeremiah was likely to face, that some good had emerged from today's events.

# CHAPTER ELEVEN

"That's three," Rod said.

"Three what?" Jeremiah asked.

Our trio was sitting in the cafeteria on Thursday, hunkered around a table like a company of Roman soldiers holding up shields to deflect a rain of arrows.

"Three people who deliberately brushed past us and swelled their chests so we couldn't miss their OnWard, UpWard T-shirts," the anesthesiologist observed. "One tech, a secretary and a nurse's aide. But who's counting?"

Jeremiah's forehead creased. "No nurses?"

"Haven't seen any yet," Rod replied. "I'm guessing they're afraid of your nurse."

"She does have a cutting edge to her tongue," I said. Celia took her loyalty seriously. "Also, her sister is gay, and they're close. Nobody can accuse her of siding against Ward from prejudice."

"I'm not prejudiced, either," Jeremiah pointed out.

"Most people prefer not to be confused by facts, when colorful rantings are readily available," our companion said.

This situation stemmed, indirectly, from Soraya's article, which had played up Alison's visit to Jeremiah two nights before her death. Quotes from Mrs. Linden—"I bet they had sex that would knock your fillings out!"—had added color.

The chatty landlady had also stated, "That shrink fella said she'd done the same thing the next night with him. Just proves he ain't lying, don't it?"

I had no idea why Ward had seized on this revelation to target Jeremiah. Maybe he'd feared that, if he criticized the police for not revealing Alison's prior nocturnal activities, they might release that he'd initially lied about having had sex with her at all.

Whatever his reasoning, Radman had kicked off his next podcast by accusing Jeremiah of deliberately keeping silent in public about the liaison with Alison. He'd pontificated, "This arrogant doctor could have helped absolve me. Instead, like much of the medical establishment, he sneers at those of us who support sexual outsiders."

After this on-air assault, Jeremiah might have escaped further fury had he remained close-mouthed. Unfortunately, when contacted by Soraya for a reaction, he'd remarked that, just because one doctor chose to broadcast his every move, that didn't require others to do so.

While I considered that a mild statement, Ward had volleyed back that Alison's encounter with "this haughty physician" had so upset her, that she'd come to him, her old mentor, for "reassurance about her sexual identity."

Her what? I hadn't heard of any uncertainty regarding Alison's sexual identity, only her taste in men.

The squabble had gone downhill from there. To support his contention that Dr. Schwartz was insensitive and self-important, Radman had dug up one of Jeremiah's former nurses, who'd cited high staff turnover. This was true, owing to Jeremiah's tone deafness in personnel management prior to hiring Celia, but hardly proof of a character flaw.

Attempting to clear the air, Jeremiah had made the mistake of agreeing to talk by phone with Radman. I'd winced as I listened to the podcast. Ward had twisted everything he'd said and peppered him with confusing questions, including references to Jeremiah's supposed opposition to LGBTQ rights.

"As a doctor, of course I'm concerned about those people," Jeremiah had said. Anyone aware of his naïveté would understand what he meant, but all Radman heard—or pretended to hear—were the words, "those people," which he'd repeated often and loudly, as if it were an insult. Since then, Jeremiah had endured threatening phone calls, patient cancellations, and open snubs.

"I do not understand why members of the medical staff accept his statements at face value and believe it is sufficient justification to insult a colleague," Jeremiah said.

"They're what my wife calls Twippages," Rod replied.

I indulged him. "What's that?"

"Those Who Pass Judgment," he said. "I prefer to call them Knee Jerks."

It was kinder than the names I might use.

A ripple of movement caught my attention. Between tables, a six-foot-tall woman with dramatic maroon hair cut toward us, arriving at the same time as a fellow puffing out his rainbow-striped OnWard, UpWard T-shirt.

"There are patients in this cafeteria," she snapped at the young man. "You're a professional. Act like one."

"Sorry, Dr. Brennan." He slunk off.

"Results already?" I asked.

"Pardon?" At my sister-in-law's request, Paige had arranged for Tory's BRCA test three days ago. But even had the results been available this fast, she would have had to maintain patient confidentiality.

"Never mind," I said. "Please join us."

"Thanks. I'm not here to eat." She regarded Jeremiah. "I thought you should know, there are pickets outside. The administration has asked them to avoid blocking patients, but you might encounter them."

Fantastic. We'd have to run a gauntlet to reach our offices.

"Is the press here?" Jeremiah asked.

"Yes, they are."

"And Radman?" I put in.

"He wouldn't miss an opportunity to grandstand," Paige confirmed. "Good luck." Our friendly informant moved on.

"Options?" Rod provided his own answer. "I might have a Spiderman costume left from Halloween so you can sneak past them. Glad to loan it to you for a small fee, Jer."

"Appearing foolish would not be wise," opined the doctor in question. "Oh. You were employing humor."

"Indeed."

"I'll walk with you." I picked up my tray.

"You are a good friend," Jeremiah said.

Guilt pricked. I hadn't been a good friend for most of the decade and a half I'd known him.

Outside in the cool early afternoon, my senses registered swarms of motion. The normal drifts and eddies of cars navigating the circular drive had been joined by a news van, perched in a green zone. In the reserved parking area between the hospital and the office building, about a dozen protesters circled with signs. "Down with bigot doctors!" was among the kindest.

To my disgust, many of them wore masks, of the medical variety. Not a very good disguise, but when had the custom grown popular of protesters acting like cowards, hiding their faces? Despite the hovering presence of two security guards on the perimeter, I felt on the firing line, passing this crowd with Jeremiah.

"Dr. Darcy!" yelled a voice of indeterminate gender. "Surely you aren't protecting this bigot!"

My fingers itched to rip off the person's mask and reveal whoever was underneath. However, it might be a patient. Or a lawyer.

"He's never said anything bigoted in my presence," I answered.

Spotting Jeremiah, the rest of the picketers broke formation. One masked woman in jeans darted forward to confront him. "You're evil! Nothing but a hater!" she shrieked. "You should die horribly!"

Hater, indeed.

"Please remove the mask," my companion said. "I will be happy to speak with you."

Another picketer—to her credit, she wasn't in disguise—waved her sign: "Love Us Or F.U." "We shouldn't have to tolerate doctors like you in the community."

"To us, *you're* 'those people,' " someone else spat out. "Trash!"

Ward certainly attracted high-class followers.

A TV cameraman captured the event, as did a news photographer festooned with cameras. From the sidelines, Soraya regarded the scene with a disgruntled expression. Her place in the spotlight had been stolen by a man with a mic, whom I recognized as TV reporter Hayden O'Donnell.

Scanning the area, I noted Radman's expensive convertible slanted across two reserved parking spaces. No sign of the man himself.

"Dr. Schwartz, is it true you've been receiving death threats?" O'Donnell asked

"No," Jeremiah said.

I couldn't believe this numbskull was putting ideas into people's heads. "Where'd you hear that rumor?" I demanded, despite an inner voice warning me to stay the hell out of this. "Did you invent it?"

His square face flushed. Hard to believe it was shame, which has gone the way of eight-track tapes and fallout shelters. "It's a reasonable question," he insisted.

Jeremiah laid a hand on my arm. "This is not your battle, Eric."

"Hey, doc," somebody sneered at him. "Better not touch the guy. People might think you're a homo."

"That would not concern me," Jeremiah said.

On our left, the hospital's staff entrance discharged a bull of a man. A touch of the doorframe for stability, plus sweat standing out on Ward Radman's face, indicated to me that something was amiss. I'd have laid bets he'd gone inside to use the restroom. Weak bladder, or a nervous stomach?

Any concerns for his health vanished as he straightened his shoulders and boomed at those gathered, "Thank you for joining me. The forces arrayed against us can see that we are united. Power to our people!"

Cheers erupted, and picketers surged toward Jeremiah and me. A couple of the signposts ended in wicked points, I registered with apprehension, and the security guards were unarmed.

In the doorway behind Radman appeared another man, even taller and more muscular. Storm clouds replaced the hospital administrator's usually affable expression. Mark Rayburn, M.D., served as a father figure to many of us, but his real baby was Safe Harbor Medical Center, and it was being violated.

"Dr. Radman, may I remind you that you do not have admitting privileges at this facility." His deep voice overrode the clamor. "You are interfering with the safety and care of our patients. Please remove yourself from these premises and end this disturbance immediately."

Ward's mouth twitched. While he must hate that the administrator had stolen his thunder, he could hardly object.

"Why does this place let a redneck doctor like him practice here?" The masked woman who hated haters gestured at Jeremiah.

"If you wish to file a complaint against one of our doctors, you may do so at the front desk," Mark responded.

"Typical bureaucrat!" shouted a picketer.

"I'll bet you'd act differently if you were transgender!" someone else declared.

The protesters shuffled about angrily, uncertain whether to aim their wrath at Mark or Jeremiah. It was a volatile moment. When individuals join a mob, they lose their normal inhibitions.

What Ward should have done was to repeat his thanks for their support and declare that they should disband out of consideration for the patients. Instead, he strode to his car, drawing his masked band with him. Preparing, in my opinion, for a dramatic exit.

"What should we do, Dr. Radman?" someone asked.

"Take pride in your identity!" He raised his arms. "We will not be defeated!"

"OnWard! UpWard!" The chant arose.

"We should leave," I told Jeremiah. "We have patients waiting." Not to mention that we were standing in the potential line of fire.

"Agreed."

That was why, as I later explained to Keith and other officers, the two of us had turned our backs a moment before Ward's car exploded.

# CHAPTER TWELVE

People running. Screaming. Dodging. Aiming their cell-phone cameras.

Jeremiah and I scurried around the corner of the building. "What the hell?" I said.

"We must postpone our patients," my colleague observed. "It is our duty to assist."

"Agreed." As doctors, we weren't about to duck an emergency, even at the risk of a second bomb. I peered into the parking area, afraid of finding an impact crater and a scattering of motionless victims.

No one lay on the pavement. Instead, people were staggering or sitting, stunned. The only wounds in view were cuts and bruises.

Ward's convertible hadn't vaporized, although the ripped interior glittered with glass. The psychiatrist leaned against a building, pale and wide-eyed. Blood dripped along his face and neck. Not enough to indicate he was in immediate danger, and when Jeremiah approached, Ward waved him off.

Was he letting personal animosity interfere with receiving care? If he'd suffered a concussion, he might not be thinking rationally. Still, plenty of other people needed assistance, and paramedics would be arriving soon.

In the doorway, the administrator was phoning for help. For once, I wished Safe Harbor had an emergency room.

"What blew up the car?" Soraya addressed her photographer, a few yards from us. "Could you tell what it was, Duncan?"

The chunky man fiddled with a camera setting. "My guess is a small explosive in a bottle. Nasty business. In case you hadn't noticed, there's glass in your hair."

"A bomb in a bottle?" She retrieved a mirror from her purse and removed the offending particle. "Like a Molotov cocktail?"

"Basically, yes."

"You seem to have experience with the subject," I observed.

"Misspent youth." Duncan resumed picture-taking. The TV cameraman was doing the same, despite a cut on his temple.

Across the narrow lot, Ward spoke into his cell. To whom? The press was already here, and the police soon would be.

"Dr. Darcy, you have a cut." Soraya held up her mirror.

Immediately, I registered a stinging sensation in my neck. Reaching up, I plucked out a small shard and tossed it into a trash container. "Thanks." Medical personnel grow accustomed to minor injuries in the daily course of our jobs.

Jeremiah, Mark Rayburn and I pitched in to help the wounded. Nurses hurried to assist, bringing bandages and first-aid supplies.

As we passed among the victims, treating the more serious wounds and checking vital signs, I wondered who had done this. Was there a remote detonation device, or had the guilty party been present?

I hadn't seen anyone running or acting strangely, but he or she could have slipped out unnoticed. Whoever had done this must have been aware that Radman owned an open car, and didn't care if bystanders got hurt.

He or she had run a risk, detonating the device in public. Sometimes, I supposed, that was the best place to hide, especially when many of the protesters wore masks.

What was the bomber's purpose? To hurt the man, or merely scare him? Was it a hate crime? It might even have been a misguided attempt to arouse sympathy for him. While there was an outside chance Ward had staged this himself, he could have suffered serious damage, such as to his eyes.

In my opinion, those masks had aided the attacker. However, they'd also served a useful purpose; some of them bristled with glass bits. Not without grumbling, the marchers took them off to be examined.

"Folks, please don't disturb things any more than you have to," Mark announced. "Let's not forget this is a crime scene."

"Like the police will care who attacked Dr. Radman," someone grumbled.

Another shrill comment drew my attention. "I don't want him touching me!" The lady who hated haters grimaced at Jeremiah, who had crouched near her on the pavement. Blood trickled down her face from a scalp wound.

The administrator regarded her sternly. "This doctor is trying to help you, but you have the right to refuse medical attention. Is that what you're doing?"

"I want *him* instead!" She indicated me.

Since she didn't seem badly hurt, I had no intention of letting her boss me around. "Dr. Schwartz is perfectly capable of treating you." Deliberately, I stepped away.

She folded her arms. "I'll wait for the paramedics."

Jeremiah joined me. "I shall notify my nurse to explain the delay."

"Good idea." I phoned my office, too, adding that I wasn't sure how soon I'd be free. With sirens wailing toward us, the paramedics should arrive any minute, but the police would want my statement, along with everyone else's.

"We heard the blast," Farrah said in my ear. "Are you okay, Dr. Darcy?"

I touched my neck. The blood was clotting nicely. "Yes."

"Shall I reschedule everyone?"

I hated inconveniencing them. "Tell the patients what's going on. If they prefer to reschedule, fine. I'll get there as soon as I can."

"Dr. Levin hasn't left for his golf game yet," she said. "I could ask him to fill in."

"Great idea. Tell him I'd appreciate it." I rarely asked favors of my partner.

Across the lot, Ward was shaking his head, perhaps in reaction to ringing in the ears. His expression fluctuated between irritation and a phony smile for the TV camera. It went oddly with his injuries, which included a gash on his cheekbone wide enough to benefit from a plastic surgeon's skills.

"Do you consider this an attempt to silence you?" Hayden O'Donnell was asking.

"Absolutely!" Radman said. "You see to what lengths my enemies will go."

Soraya broke in. "You can hardly blame this on Dr. Schwartz. He was standing over there."

"It's more Nurse Cornello's type of underhanded..." The psychiatrist broke off. "I'm not stating an accusation. The truth will emerge!" The guy had a talent for rallying when the spotlight fixed on him.

We were spared any further tirades by the flash and blare of emergency vehicles. Soon those who required additional treatment, primarily for eye injuries and deep cuts, were trundled off to Heights View Medical Center, a few miles inland. An officer secured the scene, separating the witnesses for questioning and isolating the blast zone around the car.

As crime scene technicians went about their tasks, Keith strode up. He speared me with an unsympathetic glance. "You again. Real gift for being on the spot."

"I work here," I reminded my friend.

"Well, hang loose. Somebody will take your statement."

No use arguing. Staying out of the path of the paramedics, I lingered, feeling anything but loose.

Keith went to speak to Radman. The psychiatrist's expression kept shifting, from deference to annoyance to what I interpreted as fear. While this might simply be a reaction to the explosion, he'd seemed off-center earlier as well. Was this an increasingly severe indication of trauma? If so, was it from discovering Alison's body in bed beside him, or from murdering her?

To my surprise, my sister-in-law showed up. With barely a nod to me, Tory surveyed the scene and began photographing it. She must have been summoned either by Ward or by his lawyer.

Once I finished providing a statement to a uniformed officer, Tory approached, eyebrows drawn together. "You okay?"

"Fine."

She touched the cut on my neck. "It's practically healed." Gruffly, she added, "I should have known you'd escape with barely a scratch."

"Lucky for me."

"Yeah. Dr. Teflon, as usual."

Relations had been edgy between us the past few days. On Ward's behalf, Tory had prodded me to reveal whatever I knew about Jeremiah. I'd ordered her to cut it out, that I refused to betray a friend.

"Since when is Dr. Schwartz your friend?" she'd demanded,

to which I'd replied, "Since he took a stand against a sociopathic rapist, otherwise known as your client."

She'd viewed my refusal to cooperate as ungrateful, since she was the one digging into Lydia's mystery contact. But aside from the fact that Lydia had been her sister as well as my wife, this wasn't a case of swapping information. If Radman got wind of Jeremiah's schizophrenia, the damage could be irreparable.

I respected that she had a job to do. What I didn't understand was why she showed such determination to save that bastard, who was at the very moment being loaded into an ambulance, while booming that he was fine.

"He's pretty bashed up," Tory commented.

"Should have stitches," I agreed.

Keith reached us, zeroing in on my sister-in-law. "Any word?"

"About?"

"The BRCA test."

"Not yet."

"Whatever the result is, I'm here for you." Keith's chest heaved with the effort of issuing such a touchy-feely statement.

Tory didn't acknowledge the tender declaration. "How about I review whatever video you've got? I might recognize someone."

"We haven't reviewed it ourselves yet." Keith's cell sounded. Impatiently, he answered. "Yes? Oh, really?" His body language became all business. "That's confirmed, then. Thanks for updating me, Sergeant... No, he doesn't appear seriously injured."

From the sharp look he directed toward Ward, I half-expected—or hoped—he'd march over there and announce in dramatic, TV-cop fashion, "You're under arrest!" Instead, he headed off to continue the phone conversation in private. Tory cupped her ears, straining to hear, but with so much noise—

including the departure of Ward's ambulance—it was useless.

"Got patients to see," I said. "Good luck."

"Eric!"

Her voice stopped me. "Yes?"

"Do you have a passport?"

"Of course." While I'm not much of a traveler, medical conferences take place in a range of locales. "Why?"

"Tell you later. Right now, I have to check out that lady's videos." With a gleam of satisfaction at frustrating me, Tory headed toward a woman panning her phone to capture the scene.

A passport. Had she discovered who Lydia met in Israel? My chest squeezed at the prospect of finally ripping the scabs off my wife's secrets. But eager as I was to know the truth, grabbing and shaking my sister-in-law wasn't likely to yield the desired results.

Jeremiah was heading toward his office. Best to follow his example.

I spent the rest of the day not dwelling on what Tory might have learned.

# CHAPTER THIRTEEN

Evening darkness lay heavy within my empty house. Morris had informed me he'd be out catering an event, but where the hell was Tory?

I texted. "I'm home. U?" No response.

Without much appetite, I downed part of a sandwich and retired upstairs to the game room-slash-library. While Lydia had redecorated the house mostly in warm colors, she'd retained the dark woods and high shelves in this retreat, merely rearranging the books and mementoes my parents had collected on their travels. We'd added a large-screen TV and other electronics, a parquet table for board games, armchairs and a sofa.

On a normal evening, I read medical journals and left the news until the morning paper arrived. Tonight, I switched on the TV.

Ward Radman thrust his face onto a ridiculous number of channels. Picturesquely bandaged, he'd held an impromptu press conference in front of Heights View Medical Center's emergency room, declaring he was under attack. He stated that he'd barely escaped death twice—when his car exploded, and the night Dr. Alison Abrams died, as if he'd been targeted, too.

After years of relishing the role of victim by proxy, he'd finally achieved that status, or imagined he had. The distress in his voice sounded real, though.

Footage submitted by viewers revealed a chaotic scene outside Safe Harbor Medical Center. While none had caught the actual blast, the clips jerkily captured the screams and cries in its wake.

A stern anchorwoman, citing an unnamed source, stated that this near-tragedy had resulted from an explosive device capable of wreaking severe damage. Eight injuries were confirmed. Tracing the scab on my neck, I wondered if they'd counted mine.

Hayden O'Donnell's station aired Ward's hastily voiced suspicions about Brandy Cornello. It was followed by a report that she had been at work at her medical office when the detonation occurred.

Just as I was mentally awarding him credit for fact-checking, Hayden introduced a self-described spokesman for the LGBTQ community. "This appears to be an attack by a hate group," he said. "Why weren't the police providing protection?"

He expected police to be johnny-on-the-spot at a small, apparently unannounced demonstration? Irritated, I was about to hit Power but, by instinct, toggled to another channel instead.

"I'm concerned that the media is describing as a hate crime what may be a personal issue of Dr. Radman's," said a young man. "He is a publicity-seeking celebrity who does not represent all of us in the LGBTQ community, or even most of us, in my opinion. We've been subjected to a long history of discrimination, but rallying behind an opportunist like Dr. Radman is less than helpful."

Ah, a voice of reason. I was hoping to learn this sage's name when a door thumped shut on the floor below.

Morris was not a door thumper. Heading for the railing, I called, "Tory?"

"Don't pester me till I've eaten," flew back.

She'd always had a fiery personality, but rarely directed the full force of it at me. While I didn't expect the klutzy deference I'd received in high school as her big sister's boyfriend, this exceeded her ordinary don't-step-on-me attitude.

Too bad. Determined to learn what she'd discovered about Lydia, I marched downstairs.

Across the great room, I watched my sister-in-law fling her suit jacket over a kitchen chair. Chestnut hair bounced as she jerked open the refrigerator and tossed odds and ends onto the counter.

There are things a man learns, if he's smart, about dealing with feminine ill temper. Offering to listen is good. Offering to help is better.

"How about a shoulder massage?" I advanced toward her.

"No, thanks. I can handle my own tension." She rolled her shoulders, producing crackling noises.

On the plus side, she'd thanked me. That beat heaving things in my direction.

"There's ice cream in the freezer," I added, to sweeten the deal.

"Oh, sit down and quit trying to maneuver me."

"Yes, ma'am."

I took a stool at the counter. Tory smacked a sandwich together. "Guess you'd like to know why I mentioned a passport."

"It occurred to me." I waited.

"First tell me whatever secret you're hiding about Dr. Schwartz."

I hadn't counted on horse trading. "I will not."

"Why are you shielding a man you've always loathed?" She

wedged a couple of pickles onto her paper plate.

"It has nothing to do with Alison."

"I'll be the judge of that."

"It involves his medical history." I stopped there.

"Oh." She stood at the counter, picking at food. "Does it concern Dr. Abrams dropping by his place for sex?"

"No."

"Why would she do that?"

"I have no idea and I don't believe Jeremiah does, either," I said. "That's as much as I can disclose."

She wasn't finished. "Why does he hate Dr. Radman?"

I bit back the obvious reply, which was *Doesn't everyone?* "He dislikes him because Alison did, but that's as far as it went until the on-air attacks. Your client accused Jeremiah of deliberately hiding Alison's visit, which is obviously false, since he'd told the police. Your client also claimed that he's biased, which isn't true."

"None of that explains why you're acting secretive." She spoke around a mouthful of food.

"I'm not the problem here." I drummed my fingers on the counter. "Why are you anxious to clear that monster?"

"Because I think Ward Radman might be, well, not exactly innocent, but not guilty, either."

What the hell? "He drugged and raped Brandy Cornello and Alison Abrams!"

"If so, he should be prosecuted. But he's being framed for murder."

"I can't believe you're buying his crap," I said. "On what do you base that conclusion?"

"Odds and ends that don't add up." She washed down her food with a long swallow of beer.

"Like what?"

"I'm not at liberty to say. But he's genuinely afraid of being railroaded."

*He's afraid, all right. Of having to pay for being a serial rapist.* "Why do you care?"

"Don't you care what happens to your patients, even the ones who cheat on their spouses and insult your nurse?"

There are plenty of obnoxious people in the world, but those transgressions were globally different from Radman's crimes. However, since arguing would be counterproductive, I moved on. "Tell me about Lydia. What did you dig up? Who did you contact?"

In the eating-filled silence, I wondered if she was shutting me out. Eons later, she spoke. "Kibbutzniks are tough. Last time I made inquiries about Lydia's father and his relatives, the searching-for-the-truth-about-my-sister's-death business got me nowhere. This time, I went with urgently seeking family medical information. Cancer genes and all that."

"You mentioned BRCA?" That seemed odd, considering how sensitive the topic was to her. "Based on what Morris said, it's likely Lydia inherited the mutation from your mom. There's no reason to think anyone related on her father's side would be affected."

Tory shrugged. "So? I figured it might work, and it did."

Because the BRCA mutations are more common among Jewish women than others, this would be a health issue of special concern in Israel, I supposed. "And?"

"The spokeswoman shared that Lydia had a first cousin. Same last name, Silver."

There'd been jokes that, when their mother married Morris, she'd improved her status from Nelle Silver to Nelle Golden. Lydia, who'd retained her father's surname, hadn't appreciated those jibes. I'd felt honored when she switched to Darcy after our marriage.

"Male or female cousin?" I asked.

"No details," Tory said. "The woman provided an email address. That's it."

An email address wasn't much. Still, it was more than we'd had before. Initially, when Tory learned from Lydia's tour guide that her sister had met with an unknown person in Jerusalem, she'd been frustrated to discover no phone, email or other records.

"It's progress," I said.

"Assuming the address is valid." Tory was, as ever, the skeptic. "I sent a message. Haven't heard back."

"Why the secrecy, do you suppose?"

"Maybe the cousin works in security." She took another swig of beer.

"Mossad?" Israel's intelligence agency is both famed and notorious for its covert operations.

"Who knows?" Tory said. "Better get ready. If anyone's flying to Israel, it'll be you."

I hadn't thought that far ahead, to actually meeting this person myself. The questions I had about my wife were intensely, agonizingly personal.

Why had Lydia withdrawn from me in her final months and hidden her medical condition? The woman to whom I'd given my heart had abandoned me with no apparent concern. Had she stopped loving me? Had she ever truly loved me at all?

Baring my soul to a stranger would violate my carefully fortified emotional boundaries. At moments like this, my anger bordered on loathing. Not for Lydia, but for what she'd done.

"Why do you think this person would talk to me?" I asked.

"Because you're her husband and you haven't been able to come to grips with her death," she said.

"You put that in your email?"

"Also that you're losing your battle with depression."

That startled me. "This was a ploy, right? I'm not

depressed."

"Like hell you aren't!"

"Who's the doctor here?" I shot back.

"Who's the guy in denial?" She slammed her palm on the counter. "Talk to this person, if you get the chance. I'm tired of tiptoeing around you, Eric."

Our conversation had veered into the fantastical. "When did you ever do that?"

"You've been grumpy and depressed. Be honest."

Sure, I'd been upset. Who wouldn't? My wife had left me without explanation and died under murky circumstances. While I craved answers, I was otherwise coping just fine.

Aside from occasional sleeplessness. Troubled thought patterns. Inability to consider entering into a new relationship. But...

"Okay," I said. "Mildly depressed."

To my sister-in-law's credit, she didn't gloat over her victory. "Is there really ice cream?" En route to the fridge, Tory disposed of her plate and empty beer can.

"Last time I checked."

She produced a gallon container of chocolate chip. "Thank you, Dad."

"Did he leave enough to share?"

"Sure." Her phone rang. Maybe it was Morris, on his way home with more food, I hoped. My earlier skimpy repast had left a void.

Tory answered. Listened. Scowled. "I'll see what else I can find out. Yeah, I understand." Clicked off.

"Anything new in Alison's case?" I recalled that Keith had received information earlier. "Is that from the lawyer?"

"Never mind who it's from." My sister-in-law had sources. During her ten years at the police department, she'd scored a few friends. Also, she regularly stopped by the station with that universal currency, doughnuts. "The drug they recovered from Radman's house matches the one that killed her."

That could fit his claim of being framed. Or, conversely, indicate he'd intentionally dosed her. "What's next?"

"There's talk that the police will take this to the district attorney. If I can't figure out where those drugs are from, they're likely to charge him."

"He's probably guilty," I pointed out.

"He may be a jerk, but I doubt he killed her," Tory said. "It was ketamine from the street, not medical grade. Why wouldn't he use the ketamine from his office, and why leave a baggie lying around after she died? I have to identify the source."

"Surely you've been looking into that," I said.

"Yes, as have the police. No luck," she grumbled. "There are a lot of drugs floating around Southern California."

"They won't arrest him unless they think the case is solid." Or so I assumed. Charging a wealthy public figure could create a backlash, especially if he proved to be innocent. "There's also that business about her car being relocated," I added.

"He's admitted moving her body and destroying evidence." Tory shoved the uneaten ice cream back into the freezer, a sign she was upset. "You said Dr. Schwartz had a medical condition. Is it PTSD? Could he be self-medicating with ketamine?"

"No. You're grasping at straws," I said. "Jeremiah didn't kill Alison." Although he'd told me he wasn't sure about that, I couldn't see him sneaking a baggie of drugs into Ward's house and forcing or tricking Alison into swallowing a dose, no matter how delusional he'd been.

"Tell me what you know! It might help."

"Why can't you admit that drugging her fits Ward's pattern?" I said. "Brandy claims..."

"Why do you believe her? She's the other obvious suspect.

It had to be her who moved Dr. Abrams' car."

"Maybe." My phone sounded a text alert. Might be the hospital.

The number was unidentified. I tapped the screen and read: "Cn u b in Jerusalem Monday? Sry for short notice. Must depart long period." The name at the end was "C. Silver."

Just like that, everything changed.

# CHAPTER FOURTEEN

"I wish I knew how he or she got your phone number to contact you directly," Tory said, navigating the freeway en route to Los Angeles International on Saturday. I'd gratefully accepted her offer to drive me to the airport. "It wasn't from me."

"If you were right and they work for Mossad, that would explain it." I stretched my legs in the passenger seat of the green sedan that had once been Lydia's. When I slid inside, I'd imagined I caught a whiff of my wife's perfume. My brain playing tricks, no doubt.

"Or my sister gave it to them," Tory said.

Perhaps so. This cousin had interacted with Lydia in ways I couldn't yet fathom. And might have received confidences that had been withheld from me.

After I texted that I would be there, C. Silver had requested we meet for lunch. "Details later." I'd provided information about my flight and hotel, receiving a cartoon thumbs-up in response. Hardly what I'd expect from a Mossad agent.

"Sure you wouldn't prefer to join me?" Although C. Silver hadn't insisted I go alone, and I'd offered to pay Tory's cost of traveling to Israel, she'd declined. "It's not too late."

"Too busy here."

"You've been a terrific help." She'd located the guide who'd assisted my wife's small tour group, and arranged for him to meet me at Ben Gurion Airport and chauffeur me around. She'd also booked a hotel and the flight, saying I had enough to do lining up doctors to cover for me.

My partner, Isaiah, had taken the extraordinary step of canceling his Tuesday afternoon golf game to sub for me. On other days, Jeremiah and Paige were treating patients who couldn't reschedule, as well as handling my surgeries.

I'd apologized to my nurse for another in a long list of inconveniences. "It's for a good cause," Farrah had said.

Did she, too, believe I was depressed? Regardless, I'd be lost without her support, and had told her so.

How long would I stay in Israel? As short a time as possible. Although people had encouraged me to extend my visit to tour this historic land, I was in no mood for sightseeing. However, with a nearly a fifteen-hour flight each way, I couldn't avoid an absence of several days.

"I asked to go with her," Tory said out of the blue.

My thoughts had wandered. "I'm sorry. What?"

"Lydia." She steered out of the carpool lane to pass a sedan that had the impudence to drive the speed limit. "Three years ago. She seemed troubled. And I was curious to meet her extended family, if she had any."

This was news to me. "What did she say?"

"That it was *her* family, not mine. Like I didn't matter. It made me mad. That was before I understood why she always held me at arm's length, because of what happened with our parents."

Their mother had married Morris soon after her husband's suicide, and given birth to Tory a few months later. If you counted backward, it was obvious that Nelle and Morris had been having an affair while Avram was alive, a situation that might have exacerbated his suicidal tendencies. When I connected the dots for Tory, it had helped her see why her sister might have acted stand-offish toward the step-family in which she'd grown up.

Ironically, Lydia's isolation had brought us together. When we met as high-school freshmen, I'd recently lost my mother, and she'd still been grieving for a father she hardly remembered. After a single conversation, we'd bonded.

But when she announced her plans to go to Israel, she'd informed me that she had to do this alone. We'd always maintained a respectful relationship, allowing each other our space. It hadn't occurred to me to object.

"If the Silvers were her real family, where were they when I buried her?" Tory demanded. "Where was this damn cousin?"

"Lydia shut us both out," I said. "Maybe I'll finally learn why."

"And maybe you'll trip over something that tears you apart." She gripped the steering wheel.

I shrugged. "I'm not that fragile."

"Yeah?" she scoffed. "Eric, you were her rock. Mine, too. When she died, you fell apart."

My jaw worked on a protest that never emerged.

"Whatever happens, Eric, promise you'll come back."

"Of course." Why wouldn't I? I had no Israeli connections to entice me to stay. "I'll be flying home Monday night."

"Flights can be changed. Don't rush on my account. Finish your business there, once and for all."

"That's the plan," I agreed. "But I'd like to be here when you get the BRCA results. I know that scares you."

"I'm not scared." Tory scowled at a truck that was in the wrong lane.

"You're only human." I decided it was worth venturing into

119

none-of-my-business territory. "If you need support, let Keith be there for you."

"Keith's pitying me is almost worse than him cheating," Tory muttered.

"He doesn't pity you. He cares about you." Who appointed me matchmaker? Well, somebody ought to step in. "He may be an idiot, but he's an idiot who loves you."

She didn't answer, nor did I expect her to. "Text me when you land," she said. "And stay in touch while you're there."

I promised I would.

*

Whatever I'd expected on arriving in Israel, it wasn't the sense that I'd landed in an alternate Southern California. Here was a familiar mild February twilight, palm trees feathering the sky, bougainvillea bright with blossoms—and a chatty guide who drove a Toyota.

Benjamin Mizrah met me as soon as I cleared customs. Dark-haired, slim and short, he jumped up and down among the other guides, waving a hand-lettered sign that read "Dr. Darcy!!!" Yes, three exclamation points.

He steered me to an ATM to withdraw shekels—no sense changing cash when you could simply download the currency—and carried my small suitcase to his car, all the while talking nonstop.

"It is late." He gestured toward the dimming sky. "It is an hour's drive to your hotel in Jerusalem. If you are hungry, we can stop in Tel Aviv. There are many fine restaurants, and we could eat by the beach. People tell me it's like your Santa Monica."

"I ate on the plane, and I didn't sleep much. Let's head for the hotel." I was so tired, I'd barely remembered to text Tory to report landing safely. Nor was I interested in visiting a city that mirrored one right up the coast from home. "If you haven't eaten, you could grab a bite."

"Oh, I am fine."

We drove away from the airport to the accompaniment of my guide's narrative. Tel Aviv, he declared, had been established in 1909 as a Jewish suburb of the old city of Jaffa, which later became its suburb instead. Now ranked among the world's top financial centers, according to Benjamin, Tel Aviv had a population of roughly half a million, including about four thousand Christians.

He steered onto a highway much like a California freeway, including green directional signs in English as well as Hebrew. In the front seat, I was starting to doze when my guide asked, "Do you know this Dr. Radman?"

"What?" I hadn't been prepared for a mention of my least favorite psychiatrist. "How did you hear about him?"

"Tel Aviv is famous for gay friendly." He frowned. "Should I say, *as* gay friendly?"

"Yes. Or, for *being* gay friendly."

"They have erected a monument to gay victims of the Holocaust." Keeping one hand on the wheel, Benjamin waved for emphasis. "LGBTQ rights are more advanced in Israel than anywhere else in the Middle East. Although we do not perform same-sex marriages, we recognize them from other countries, and we prohibit discrimination. We serve in the military, like most citizens." His use of "we" indicated he had a personal stake in the matter.

That didn't explain why he followed my local news. "I'm surprised you've heard of Dr. Radman."

"Of course," he said. "You are from Safe Harbor, and that is where they blew up his car, yes?"

I decided against sharing that I'd been a witness. "That's right. The police haven't identified the culprit. Dr. Radman seems to be fine."

"We have many opinions about him." In the twilight, the highway was well lit. "Do you believe he killed the lady? Or is he framed?"

"I don't have a clue," I said. "Where are we, exactly?"

He reverted to tour mode. "We will soon be passing through the Judean Mountains. Parts of this highway follow a historic path between Jaffa and Jerusalem. We will pass rusted military vehicles beside the road. They are preserved to commemorate their role in trying to break the siege of Jerusalem during the War of Independence in 1948."

"Both our nations had wars of independence." I'd automatically associated that title with events in my own country. Rather parochial of me, I decided.

"However, the British do not call their defeat at your hands the Catastrophe, *Al-Nakba,* as the Palestinian Arabs do theirs," Benjamin commented. "About seven hundred thousand of them fled, losing their homes and businesses, and many still live in refugee camps in neighboring countries. After the war, seven or eight hundred thousand Jews were stripped of their property and expelled from other countries in the Middle East, and fled here. It never seems to equal out, though."

Since I had no wisdom to contribute, I changed the subject. "Why did you decide to be a guide?"

His family owned a travel bureau, Benjamin told me. He enjoyed learning about other cultures and religions. Most of the tourists he escorted were either Jews or Christians. "Muslims prefer their own guides."

In the near darkness, I stared at scrubby brushlands that reminded me once again of California. Biblical battles had been fought across these hills. Hard to grasp that they'd been trampled by armies of Romans, Persians, Babylonians and Sumerians, or was I thinking of Assyrians?

*Get to the point, Eric.* "Do you remember my wife, Lydia?

She took one of your tours a couple of years ago."

"I do," he said. "An intense lady. She kept to herself. I believe the others were strangers to her."

"That's right." According to Tory, she'd signed up to join a group through a travel agent. "What else do you remember?"

"Well, as I told your, what, stepsister?"

"Sister-in-law."

"I can never keep those words straightened," he said. "As I told your sister-in-law, she contacted someone in Jerusalem. Now this person is in touch with you, no?"

"She or he is supposed to text me the location of our lunch meeting tomorrow." I refrained from noting that the situation struck me as ridiculously hush-hush. What might constitute excessive caution in the U.S. could be normal here.

"Since you will be free in the morning, where will you like to go?" Benjamin promptly answered his own question. "For a Christian, the most important places are the Via Dolorosa and the Church of the Holy Sepulchre, the spot where Jesus died and was buried. It is your holiest site. That is Jerusalem's gift and its curse, that it is holy to three great religions."

I refrained from explaining that I wasn't very Christian. "I suppose I should." Maybe I would experience a religious epiphany. What if this journey transformed my life in ways I hadn't anticipated? And didn't want, either. Nevertheless, I agreed to put Holy Sepulchre on the itinerary.

"Tomorrow afternoon, I must visit my wife's grave." I named the cemetery. "Is it far from Jerusalem?"

"Not far," Benjamin said.

Despite my reluctance, I had to ask the next question. "Were you present when Lydia died?"

He shook his head. "Our tour did not include Masada. I believe she went on her own."

"She drove? How far?"

"Two hours from Jerusalem," Benjamin said. "The highway runs between the Dead Sea and the West Bank."

That meant it skirted Palestinian territory. "Isn't it dangerous?"

"The highway is safe. Perhaps she took the bus," Benjamin said. "It is easy to do if you are adventurous."

*Or determined.* She'd chosen to make her final journey alone. Only because she detested having other people intrude on her thoughts? Or had she been resolved to die and didn't want anyone stopping her?

"I was shocked to learn of her death," he added. "I am sorry. I wish to have prevented it, but what could I do? We do not talk much about suicide in Israel. It is a terrible thing, the most common reason for death among our soldiers, more than any other cause. I don't know why."

"I thought my wife's fall was ruled an accident."

"Yes. Sorry. I forgot."

His comment about the soldiers reminded me of what Alison's brother had said about the impact of the Holocaust on descendants of survivors. There could be other reasons for despair, though. Suicides occurred in my country and among our soldiers, too.

What seemed a short while later, Benjamin stopped the car at a viewpoint. "You must get out to see Jerusalem," he said. "Although you are tired, you will be glad."

No sense arguing, although my body ached, and the few steps to the low wall felt like a hike. Then I lifted my eyes and stood transfixed.

Below me glowed a city both alien and resonant, as if the entire world centered on its golden dome. Around the gleaming structure spread low roofs, walls and towers that might have been lifted from a medieval painting. Once again, I perceived the heavy weight of centuries and civilizations, the thunder of boots and the whisper of sandals. For a moment, I lost my sense of who I was.

"That is the Dome of the Rock." Benjamin's voice drew me from my wandering, as he indicated the golden structure that dominated the city. "Built in the late seventh century, the mosque sits on the rock from which the Prophet Muhammad ascended to heaven. It is also believed to be the place where God ordered the patriarch Abraham to sacrifice his son, Isaac, as a test of faith. Luckily, God called it off."

He soothed my turmoil with these facts or legends or whatever they were. "When was this? I mean, if anyone can figure it out."

"Scholars say Abraham lived roughly four thousand years ago," Benjamin replied.

My brain stretched to accommodate the concept of four millennia. The phrase "mists of time" floated up. Or was I just foggy from jet lag?

My guide resumed his account. The rock had become the Temple Mount, the site of King Solomon's temple until it was destroyed by the Babylonians. Later, a second temple on the site was destroyed by the Romans, leaving only the Western Wall, known as the Wailing Wall because people wept there as they recited prayers. To Jews, it was the most sacred structure in the world.

He went on about how the present walls of the Old City had been built by the Ottoman sultan Suleiman the Magnificent in the fifteen hundreds. I must have swayed on my feet.

"We had better go," said my guide. "You are bigger than me and if you collapse, I cannot carry you." On numb legs, I accompanied him to the car.

After weaving through modern city streets, we arrived at a multi-story hotel. Benjamin went with me to the front desk, where a clerk studied my documents and handed me an electronic key.

"Breakfast is served from 6:30 to 10 a.m.," the clerk said. "It is included with your room."

"You should not miss this," Benjamin informed me. "An Israeli breakfast is a feast."

"Great. Thanks."

He checked to be sure I had his cell number. "I will see you in the morning. Eight o'clock?"

While my instincts cried out to sleep late, I'd read that your body adjusts faster while traveling if you stick to your normal schedule. "Sure."

My suitcase and I ascended via an elevator, strayed down a hall, and let ourselves into a large room with a bathroom, a TV and, according to a card on the dresser, free WiFi.

I cleaned up in a hurry, stripped off my clothes and fell into bed. My last thought was that, tomorrow, I might finally get answers.

# CHAPTER FIFTEEN

I awoke to find a text from C. Silver. "Noon, Jaffa Gate." I confirmed with a simple "Ok."

Showered, more or less alert and stuffed from the breakfast buffet, I met Benjamin in the lobby. When I told him of the text, he said, "Jaffa Gate is the main entrance to the Old City. No doubt you will receive further instructions there."

More subterfuge. Great.

However, already my perceptions were changing. My view out the window no longer struck me as alien, while Benjamin's smiling face was familiar. As before, he wore a T-shirt bearing the travel bureau logo, but in a different color.

"Where did you sleep?" I asked.

"My agency maintains an apartment in Jerusalem," he said.

"Well-stocked with T-shirts."

"Naturally."

We navigated a short distance, parked and walked into the Old City via the Damascus Gate. It was a hike to the Church of the Holy Sepulchre through narrow streets, past shops and cafés aromatic with spices and coffee. Benjamin catalogued the sites we were passing—little of which stuck in my memory—

and described the city's divisions into Muslim, Armenian, Jewish and Christian quarters. This one, I gathered, was Christian.

The flow of visitors, of many races in a stunning array of garments, thickened as we traced the Via Dolorosa, the path that Jesus had walked to the crucifixion. Outside the Church of the Holy Sepulchre, Benjamin stopped, noting that it would be difficult to talk indoors, where services might be under way in the many shrines and chapels.

"In the past, a Muslim guard held the keys to the church to prevent fighting among Christian sects," he told me. "The primary custodians today are the Roman Catholics, the Greek Orthodox and the Armenian Apostolic churches."

Did everything become political? I wondered. But then, what had been more political down the ages than religion?

We entered the shimmering interior, ornate with golden crosses and lamps. At the Stone of the Anointing, where Jesus' body had been prepared for burial, a group of African women in long white robes prostrated themselves on the floor. Beside them knelt wide-eyed children, while a wizened old man held out his hands as if for warmth. Prayers in many languages tangled in the air, rising, presumably, to heaven.

I wished I experienced a divine presence. Whatever the state of my soul, it lay quiet here. Yet I perceived the glory of divinity in these worshippers, and envied them a little.

It was after nine when we left. "Is there anything nearby that was important to my wife?" I asked.

"That would be Yad Vashem," Benjamin said. "The Holocaust Museum."

While we had such a museum in Los Angeles, I'd never gone. Films and documentaries had told me plenty about that tragedy. "You think it would provide insight into Lydia's frame of mind?" I hoped he'd say no.

"You must go there."

"Are you sure there's time?" A slender thread of reprieve dangled before me.

"Whatever time you have, it will be enough," Benjamin said.

I yielded. Silently, if not graciously.

A fifteen-minute drive brought us to the hillside complex. Along the route, my guide provided a running account of the site's history and design. He referred to the Holocaust as *Shoah*, which was its Hebrew name, meaning "Destruction."

"What does Yad Vashem mean?" I asked.

"It translates as `a place and a name.' That's what it provides for the millions who died without a burial, without a grave, without anyone to say the *Kaddish* prayer for the dead," he replied as he parked. "I suggest we start with the main museum."

"What else is there?" I noted multiple buildings.

"An art museum of works created during the *Shoah*, many by children," he said. "A Garden of the Righteous to honor gentiles who saved Jews. A visual center with films and video testimonials. Also..."

I cut off the list. "The main museum will be fine."

In a stream of tourists, we plunged into a dark tunnel that, my guide told me, cut through a mountain ridge. Photographs, video interviews with survivors, Nazi flags and swastikas—they surged into a river of terror.

Loudspeakers broadcast harsh commands, herding us past heaps of possessions: towers of shoes, eyeglasses and suitcases, a reminder that many of those forced to their deaths had believed they were simply being relocated. Those shoes and eyeglasses—how many had belonged to Lydia's family members, their friends and teachers and schoolmates?

"It can be hard to grasp the enormity of the *Shoah*." What a relief to discover Benjamin beside me in the dimness. "It blurs

129

in our minds, the killing of six million Jews, as if they were a formless mass. Not at all. Each was an individual murder."

The Nazi death camps had also slain another five million people: gays, gypsies, the mentally ill and the physically handicapped, he said. One of the world's most educated and sophisticated cultures had applied its advanced technology to the systematic extermination of law-abiding people, some of them veterans who'd fought for Germany in World War I.

When at last we exited, a glorious panorama spread before us. Jerusalem. For this day, we were safe.

"One more thing," Benjamin said.

I glanced at my watch. Nearly eleven. "I know there's more, but..."

"This won't take long. It was important to your wife."

I yielded.

"A married couple from Ukraine lost their two-year-old son at Auschwitz," my guide said as he led me to the Children's Pavilion, which nestled in a cavern. "After they survived and moved to America, they longed to commemorate their little boy and the other young victims."

Inside, pinpricks glowed overhead in a dark dome, like stars in the sky. Memorial candles reflected in mirrors symbolized the one and a half million murdered children, Benjamin explained.

A recording read off the names and ages and hometowns. Babies that someone had labored to give birth to. Children with inquisitive minds, smiling faces, chubby hands.

I shivered. When Lydia stood here, had everything come crashing down—her terrifying diagnosis, the curse of a genetic flaw, her yearning for children?

"We'd better go," Benjamin said.

"Yes." *Finally.*

We returned to the Old City. As instructed, we approached

via the Jaffa Gate, which for defensive purposes had to be entered via a structure at right angles to the main wall. In a flow of pedestrians, we swung into a plaza rimmed with historic structures and tourist shops.

While I scanned passersby for any hint of my contact, Benjamin gestured at two nameless stone tombs. "They're believed to hold the remains of the architects of the city walls, who were executed by Suleiman the Magnificent. One legend says he was angry that they failed to enclose David's tomb and Mount Zion within the walls. Another, that he feared they might disclose the secrets of any weak points to invaders."

*Thank you, and off with your heads.* Despite the passage of five hundred years, outrage arose on their behalf. For me, time collapsed here, where you could walk the same streets as Jesus and King David.

No one stood out among those strolling around us. Surely C. Silver would be studying us. Then I recalled Benjamin's suggestion that there would be further instructions.

With all the traffic and chatter, I couldn't hear my phone. When I drew it out, there was a text bearing the name of a restaurant.

I showed it to my guide. "That's in the Mamillah Mall," he said. "It's close by. Walking distance."

"There's a mall?" Not the kind of thing I associated with the Holy City.

"Follow me."

We exited through the gate, Benjamin's short legs hurrying to keep pace with my strides. Our destination spurred him to relate how a major nineteenth century shopping street had been destroyed during the War of Independence before being redeveloped. Mercifully, he ran short of breath, sparing me further details about Mamillah.

We reached an open-air pedestrian promenade lined with

expensive stores. Eateries abounded. Where was the one I'd been directed to? Or would there be another text, another change of location?

"Here." Benjamin led me into an upscale restaurant. As I took my bearings in the busy main room, he conversed in Hebrew with a young woman.

My heart was pounding, partly from exertion, mostly at the prospect of what might lie ahead. *Calm down, think clearly, pay attention.*

Benjamin addressed me. "This lady will take you to your table. Text me when you are finished."

"Okay. Thanks."

Amid the scents of roasted lamb and spices—among which my Morris-trained nose identified cumin, cinnamon and garlic—the hostess steered me to a patio lined with tables, most of them full. Mine was in a corner. Empty.

"I'm expecting someone."

She handed me a menu. "They will be here shortly. Do you care for wine?"

"Water, thank you."

Did her use of the plural pronoun "they" mean more than one person was coming? I struggled not to overthink this.

Around me, conversations buzzed and dishes rattled. A group of women laughed together. A man waved his fork for emphasis as he spoke.

Where was Lydia's cousin?

My phone rang. *Oh, hell. Not a delay.*

It wasn't C. Silver; it was Tory. Given the ten-hour time difference, she must have been worried to contact me in the middle of the night.

I should have let her know my status, I conceded, and reined in my impatience. "I'm at a restaurant, waiting for Mr. or Ms. Silver. What's up?"

"I couldn't sleep," said that familiar voice, as sharply as if she were in the next room rather than halfway around the globe. "The news media found the counselor who treated Dr. Abrams in Azalea Springs. She says Alison claimed Ward Radman raped her."

"That counselor's breaking the law." The government bars care providers from releasing identifiable health information until fifty years after a patient's death.

"She insisted on anonymity, not that that makes it legal." A rough edge reflected Tory's stress. "Anyway, the cat's out of the bag. A couple of other women have made similar accusations."

"How're Radman's supporters taking it?" I watched a newly arrived couple trail the hostess to a table. Well-dressed and middle-aged, they seemed intent on each other.

"They're confused," my sister-in-law said. "He asserts he's being tried in the court of public opinion based on hearsay and gossip."

"Indeed." I didn't care if the court of public opinion nailed that creep to the wall. "Any indication if or when he'll be charged?"

"No idea," Tory said. "Besides, I wasn't hired to assist in his defense for rape. Murder's another story."

"I thought you were hired to dig up the truth." Since the patio could be accessed from several interior doors, with frequent movement by serving staff, it was hard to keep tabs.

"That's what I'm doing," she replied. "I think he was drugged that night. The baggie really may have been planted. I haven't been able to trace where the drugs were obtained. If he goes down, it shouldn't be because of my negligence."

"You're doing your best."

"Am I?"

Another door opened to the patio. "I'm sure you are."

Then I stopped talking, because my wife had just walked in.

# CHAPTER SIXTEEN

"Eric?" Tory's voice rattled in my ear.

"Gotta go. She's here. You get some sleep." I clicked off.

The woman studied me across the bustling patio. Caught my gaze and nodded.

She was Lydia from another universe. A little taller, her coloring lighter, but the set of her shoulders, the tilt of the head, and the flow of her hair belonged to my wife.

The gait was different, though. Flatter, braced for action. She wore tailored slacks, a multi-pocketed jacket, sturdy shoes. Her eyes swept our surroundings.

I rose to shake hands. Firm grip, a spark at the contact. We both smiled at the random electricity.

"I'm Chava Silver." The woman took a seat.

So that was what the "C" stood for. It was a guttural "ch" sound, as much an "h" as a "k." "Eric Darcy." After the jolt of seeing her, I had to draw a few breaths.

"I recommend the Israeli cuisine." She didn't sound like Lydia, and not because of the slight accent. Her tone was less husky, more cultured. "Shall I order for us both?"

"Please do."

She handled the business swiftly. As the young male server

stood before us, she took his measure. I could almost read the mental catalog of height, weight, age, mole on the right cheek.

"Thank you for seeing me," I said after he vanished.

"You have questions." She regarded me levelly.

In meeting a stranger, normally we indulge in polite chitchat. Neither of us would bother with that. Yet, this wasn't an interrogation, either. More like a physical exam, with the goal of a diagnosis.

I started at the beginning. "Why did Lydia come to Israel? Why did she seek you out?"

"She didn't give you a reason?" Answering a question with a question.

"To learn about her family history," I said. "What happened to her grandparents. Why it haunted her father. Why he killed himself." Too many points, but I let her sort them out.

"If her father had stayed to fight for his country, perhaps... " She tapped on the table, then stilled her fingers. "I will tell you what I told her."

Their grandparents, she said, had been German, the grandfather an optometrist like Lydia's father. They'd fled to the Netherlands, only to be overtaken by the Nazi invasion. Righteous gentiles had hidden them, but soon everyone in the country was starving. Neighbors noticed the good people taking extra food and reported them. The Silvers had been captured along with their brave protectors, whose fate Chava had never learned.

How had the grandparents survived imprisonment? "They were young. They were put to work of some sort." They had been beaten and starved, and near death when the Allies liberated them.

Separated, the couple had believed each other lost forever. After the war, they'd met by chance in a displaced persons camp.

If they sought to return to their native countries, the quarter of a million Holocaust survivors had faced violence and even murder by those who'd seized their businesses and homes, Chava related. Also, most nations closed their borders to the refugees. When they sought to emigrate to Palestine, the British, who'd controlled the region since the collapse of the Ottoman Empire after World War I, had barred them entry.

"They were stateless," she said. "Sympathizers and Zionist groups scrounged up a few ships. Despite blockades, risking their lives, our grandparents reached Palestine."

She paused as the server slid plates in front of us. Without reacting to whatever he'd overheard—it must be a common story here—he ensured that we required nothing else, and left.

In their new land, the traumatized pair had led a hardscrabble existence in a kibbutz named Kfar Etzion, an agricultural commune on arid land. They'd had two sons, Moshe—Chava's father—and, a year later, Avram.

In the face of competing factions and rising violence, the United Nations had ended the British Mandate and approved a partition of Palestine, attempting to carve out roughly equal territories for Jews and Arabs, with Jerusalem under international control.

The Jewish Agency for Palestine had accepted the plan. The Arab occupants rejected it. As soon as the British withdrew, the land was invaded by Arab forces from surrounding nations.

"Kfar Etzion had the misfortunate to sit on the ancient highway to Jerusalem." Chava ate quickly, in small bites between sentences. In the war, almost all of the four hundred and fifty kibbutzniks, many tattooed with dark-blue numbers from their Nazi imprisonment, had died.

The Silvers were among them. Their baby sons survived because a friend had taken them to a safer kibbutz.

"Lydia's father never knew his parents?" I hadn't been

aware of that.

"No," Chava said. "My father retained a single photo of them. They had hollow, haunted faces."

"Who raised the boys?"

"They grew up in the children's house," she said. "The kibbutzniks looked after them, but according to my dad, they didn't form close attachments."

What a terrible situation for two young children. "They had each other, though, right?"

She shrugged. "It was a link, but also a competition. Avram had more academic smarts, a chance to go to university in America, and when he was eighteen, he left. For good."

"Did they stay in touch?"

"No. They argued bitterly. Papa never forgave him for abandoning Israel." Chava spoke in a clipped manner. "When war broke out soon afterwards, in 1967, we feared we would lose our land. Although we won, there has been more warfare. A surprise invasion in 1971. Many losses." Her words tumbled out. "We live surrounded by enemies. Look at a map, how small we are. And still Jews immigrate, needing refuge. Only because Israel exists do we not have more mass slayings. And we protect minority faiths like the Druze and the Baha'i."

I had heard views in the United States about Palestinian suffering. But I wasn't here for a political debate. "Is your father alive?"

"He died five years ago."

"I'm sorry."

"He smoked too much. After a suicide bomber killed my mother at their niece's wedding, he lost his purpose. He was ready to go."

Her plate was nearly empty. I had to hurry. "Did Lydia tell you about her medical issues?"

"The ovarian cancer and the BRCA mutation? Yes."

"Since it was apparently on her mother's side, you shouldn't be affected," I said. "We aren't even certain she had cancer. She postponed the biopsy."

My companion frowned. "This I did not know."

"Neither did I." Anger laced my words. "About any of it. Even that she'd seen a specialist. She didn't tell her own husband she might be dying. I thought we were close."

Chava glanced at a couple of men in business suits walking toward us between tables. I imagined I could read her mind: Why weren't they accompanied by the hostess? They passed us and joined a group already seated.

She lost interest in them. "How did you meet my cousin?"

"At school, when we were fourteen," I said. "My mom had died the previous year. Having also lost a parent, she understood me better than anyone."

"Ah." She blinked. "I just remembered something she said. About your mother."

"*My* mother? Lydia never met her."

"About your father, really."

My wife had been well acquainted with Dad; at his invitation, we'd shared his house for three years before a heart attack felled him. "What was that?"

"He never forgave himself for failing to insist his wife get mammograms, and here he was a doctor like you."

He'd felt guilty about that? "He used to suggest them. Mom refused." Devoted to holistic living, exercise, and organic foods, she'd rejected the notion that she might fall prey to breast cancer.

"He told Lydia it haunted him," Chava said.

How strange, that such a conversation had taken place between my father and my wife, while I remained oblivious. "That's why she hesitated to confide in me about her illness?"

"She worried how it might affect you," Chava said. "I told

139

her that was selfish. Of course you would find out. Such matters cannot be hidden."

"I wish she'd let me help her."

"And then she killed herself, without even a biopsy!" She steamrollered on. "It's infuriating."

"You don't believe the fall was accidental?"

"The authorities say that because they don't want to put ideas in people's heads about suicide. But my cousin—she didn't talk a lot. What went on inside her, she didn't share much. That was her personality. But that she collapsed in the heat and fell over a cliff? No. Lydia was a coward like her father. Afraid to fight."

What the hell? "You scarcely knew her! She was sensitive and vulnerable."

Chava clunked her fork onto her plate. "This 'sensitive' woman ran off and left you." The words emerged as a growl. "Abandoned her husband and sister, and kept cruel secrets. She thought only of herself. Here you are nearly three years later, still in pain, still obsessed with this woman."

"I'm not obsessed!" *Be honest.* "If I am, it's because I loved her. I'm just not sure she loved me."

"If she didn't, that was because of her flaws, not yours. We all doubt ourselves, but we don't drag our loved ones down with us." Judging by the ragged edge, Chava spoke from experience.

She was, I recalled, a person apart from her relationship to Lydia. A person who faced her own darkness. "What brought that on?"

"Nothing."

I switched tactics. "Are you married? Kids?"

"A daughter," she said. "The father was a Canadian tourist who never knew about her."

"He's her father. Doesn't he deserve to be involved?"

140

"He was gone the next morning. Didn't leave a contact number." She studied me, much as Lydia used to do. Weighing her response. "I raised Edel for a few years and then let a friend take her."

"Why?"

"I have followed a path that for me is more meaningful than family."

Protecting her country? "What kind of work do you do?"

A hint of a smile touched her mouth. "I am employed by an investment company. It requires a lot of travel."

*Is that your cover story?* "It must have been hard, leaving your daughter. How old is she?"

"Twenty-two and religious. The opposite of me. Covers her hair, follows the rabbinical rules. Married with three children. They call my friend Grandma, not me."

"You're estranged from her?"

"I would say that we live separately."

My food had disappeared, although I scarcely recalled eating it. "How did Lydia track you down?"

"Not easily," Chava responded. "Her father must have held onto information about the kibbutz."

Her criticism of my wife troubled me. "Did you and Lydia quarrel?"

"We spoke frankly," she said.

I sensed there was more to this disclosure, to her willingness to confide in a near-stranger. "Why did you agree to meet me today?"

She considered briefly. Then: "Since my fortieth birthday, I have been reviewing my choices. There are people who might be much the same but follow different paths. Where do those take them? Did they choose right? My father and Avram. Lydia and me. I was curious."

"About me?"

"Yes. What kind of man she fell in love with. Why she left you."

Tough subject, but that was why I'd journeyed here. "Your conclusions?"

"Growing up in a large, powerful country, Lydia was safe to indulge her feelings and fears. To shrug off any higher cause." Elbows on the table, Chava examined my face. "Your sister-in-law says you care deeply about your patients, and you have traveled halfway around the world because you can't stop loving your wife. Conclusion? She chose wrong, to die alone."

"Not in marrying me?" I asked wryly.

"I doubt she ever thought that," Chava said. "Now, I must go. Perhaps I have talked too much. That is rare for me."

"I gathered that."

I stood when she did. Her handshake was strong and businesslike. As she strode away between tables, I no longer had the sense of seeing my wife, but a woman whose lineage had branched off from hers long ago.

The idea was simplistic, that Avram had been weak and had passed that to his daughter. I didn't accept it. Nor was it simply a matter of growing up in different countries. Genes, epigenes, culture, childhood, individual personality, and Lydia's relationship with me had factored in as well.

After paying, I met my guide outside the restaurant. "Did you get answers?" he asked.

Had I? "Mostly, I got opinions."

"Well, we *are* Jewish," Benjamin said. Whatever that meant.

We drove to the cemetery. There was plenty of time; my flight didn't leave until late that night. Benjamin, who'd assisted Tory with the funeral arrangements, showed me through the tightly packed rows of white headstones to the one engraved with my wife's name.

Despite the surrounding pine trees and bits of greenery and

flowers, the place seemed austere. Her headstone was well-kept—I paid a private organization called a *chevra kadisha* or holy society to maintain it—but cold.

"It's not what I expected," I said.

"Green expanses?" Benjamin asked. "Impractical. We're a tiny country with many dead. Also, cremation violates traditional Jewish belief."

I had to admit, I'd visualized the rose garden in our rear yard, bathed in a late-afternoon glow. Or a pleasant sweep like the place where Alison had been laid to rest. "I just attended a Jewish funeral," I said. "For Dr. Abrams. The lady Dr. Radman might have killed."

"Different from this," he guessed. "You knew her?"

"Professionally," I said. "I hadn't been aware that Lydia was Dr. Abrams' patient. They shared information that I knew nothing about."

"Do *your* patients share their secrets?" Benjamin asked.

I gathered he meant beyond symptoms and medical histories. "As their physician, it's my duty to ask about marital relations and watch for signs of abuse."

"To be a doctor, it's like a bartender." The young man eased aside, clearing passage for an elderly man with a cane. "Your customers talk freely. What happens in a bar, stays in a bar, isn't that the saying?"

"Not exactly." The old adage concerned Las Vegas, as I recalled. Not to mention that, these days, whatever happens in Vegas shows up all over the Internet. "Medical confidences are protected by law. Conversations with bartenders, no."

"If I were a Mossad agent, I would be a bartender," Benjamin said. "Imagine what I would hear!"

"And you'd get free drinks."

"That, too. So. Did Dr. Abrams go to a bar?"

A memory pricked. Alison's partner had said she partied at

the Suncrest Saloon. "Occasionally." Surely Tory and the police had questioned the staff regarding her habits and companions. "Let's not dwell on that case, okay?"

"Yes, yes. Sure."

My mind drifted back to this place. For three years, I'd vowed to visit Lydia's grave. Whatever I'd hoped to encounter, it wasn't this blankness.

There was no sense here of my petite wife, her long dark hair and intense manner, her rainbow moods and the artistry that had bloomed in her designs. No whisper of the students she'd mentored in teaching an art class; no reminder of the laughter and teasing in our private moments.

An omission hit me. "I forgot to bring flowers."

"Flowers mean nothing to the dead." Benjamin handed me a small stone. "We place these on graves, to show that we were here. That the stories of the dead carry weight."

There'd been flowers at Alison's funeral. Different place, different mourners. Dutifully, I placed the stone on Lydia's grave. To me, it accomplished nothing.

My wife wasn't here. That meant I had to make another journey, one I dreaded.

To understand her life, I had to revisit her death.

# CHAPTER SEVENTEEN

On the two-hour drive to Masada, I put in a call to Tory. After some odd carrier switching by my phone, which got confused as to whether I was in Israel or Jordan, I reached her to say that I had postponed my flight until tomorrow.

"Tell me what you learned from Lydia's cousin." Despite a trace of gravel in her voice, urgency infused her words. She didn't complain about my calling at roughly 6 a.m. California time.

With Benjamin at the wheel, listening, I recounted our conversation. The tragedies of the grandparents, the alienated brothers, Chava's insistence that Lydia's death had been suicide.

"You believe her?" my sister-in-law asked.

"I wish I didn't," I said. "I have to see the place for myself. How're things there?"

"Heating up, according to this morning's paper," she said.

"Heating up how?"

"Several more women are contending that Dr. Radman drugged and sexually assaulted them," she replied.

"Recently?"

"Years ago, in Azalea Springs. He claims it's a conspiracy."

"What kind of conspiracy?"

"Because of his support for gays and trans and so on," she said. "There *are* plenty of bigots posting hate stuff online."

"You can't believe he's innocent." I stared out the window at the curving coastline and the blue waters of the Dead Sea. Benjamin had noted earlier that it was literally dead, unable to support life because of its extremely high salinity. Due to the density, you couldn't swim in it, either. You could, however, sit or lie down and bob effortlessly on the surface, an activity popular among tourists. Not tempting, in my present mood.

"Innocent of rape? No. But nothing points conclusively to murder," she said.

My guide, who'd been wiggling impatiently, burst out, "Ask your sister-whatever, has Dr. Radman been arrested?"

Since Tory must have heard, I clarified, "Benjamin's following the case." I assumed she knew who I meant, since she'd hired him.

"He hasn't been arrested," she said, "although the police and D.A. are under a lot of pressure to act."

I regarded Benjamin sternly. "The answer is No, and please keep your eyes on the road."

"I am an excellent driver," he huffed. "Did you ask her about the bartender?"

"What bartender?" Tory said.

"Benjamin has a theory that the guy at the Suncrest Saloon might have overheard an important clue," I told her. "Because people talk freely in front of bartenders."

"Your guide watches too many detective shows," she grumbled. "I've talked to the staff there. As have the police, I'm sure."

"She's way ahead of you," I relayed to my driver. Since my head was starting to spin, I put the phone on Speaker. "Okay, now you two can hear each other."

"Did you ask the bartender if he has any idea who blew up her car?" Benjamin said.

"I asked him a lot of things." Irritation crept into Tory's tone. "He denies knowing  know anything except what he's seen on TV."

"If I ran a bar, I would keep my mouth shut, too," he said.

Tory didn't respond. I guessed her thoughts ran along the lines of: Why don't you keep your mouth shut *now*?

Instead, she changed the subject. "When's your new flight?"

I provided the particulars, and that was that.

Benjamin resumed his guide duties. "The land here is the lowest spot on the planet, about four hundred meters—that's thirteen hundred feet—below sea level. The Dead Sea is saltier than your Great Salt Lake in Utah. About thirty-three percent salinity, compared to about twenty-seven percent."

Fascinating. Or not.

After a while, we turned off the highway and ascended a plateau into a dry, harsh landscape. With darkness falling, Benjamin informed me that Masada National Park had closed for the night. Whatever truths it held about my wife would have to wait for daylight.

"Although the weather is cool, I presume you will prefer to ride the cable car tomorrow," he said as we neared the hotel I'd booked.

"What's the alternative?"

"The Snake Path is a forty-five minute gradual trek," Benjamin said. "There is also an ancient path along a ramp built by the Romans. It is a twenty-minute climb, but rather steep."

"How high is this mountain?"

"Thirteen hundred feet."

Roughly as high as the Dead Sea was deep, I mused. "I

choose option number one."

"Sensible." Navigating around tour buses bearing placards in German, English and Japanese, he zipped into a parking space.

"Where are you staying?" I asked.

"My agency has an arrangement."

Of course they did.

Later, dining alone in the hotel restaurant, I was vaguely aware of chatter around me, in multiple languages. Despite the buses, the place wasn't crowded in the off-season. No one intruded on my solitude.

What if I didn't find answers tomorrow? What if I detected no trace of my wife's presence? I might never truly understood how or why she'd died.

I recalled Chava's reference to alternative life paths. What would mine have been, if I had never connected with Lydia?

Strange to consider that I might not have met Morris or Tory. Scratch that; Tory had dated Keith, my best friend, but she wouldn't be living in my house. There'd be no trotting downstairs to discover Morris and my brother-in-law fixing omelets in the kitchen, either. I might know Barry as a colleague, but distantly. The urologists at Safe Harbor had offices in a separate, recently remodeled building.

Without Tory operating as a private detective out of Lydia's old studio, I doubted I'd have landed in the midst of Ward's case, either. On second thought, that might have been a plus.

Who would I have married? A fellow medical professional like Alison? What a weird notion. I must be falling asleep on my feet or, in this case, my butt.

I went to my room, slept soundly, and remembered none of my dreams.

*

En route to the national park, Benjamin explained that the

mountaintop fortress had been built around 30 B.C. by the notorious King Herod the Great. He was one of those historical figures who combined great ability—as a politician and a builder, including the Second Temple in Jerusalem—with an evil, paranoid personality. He'd murdered anyone he viewed as a threat, including his wife and sons.

According to the Bible, when Jesus was born, Herod had ordered a massacre of newborn males around Bethlehem to thwart a prophecy about a future King of the Jews. Worried that the population would rise against him, the ruler had commissioned this isolated sanctuary built over three rock terraces in the Judean Desert, equipped for a siege with weapons, storehouses and cisterns to catch rainfall.

But it wasn't the king who'd taken refuge here, Benjamin said. Around 70 A.D., long after Herod's death, Jews had rebelled against the Roman conquest, and lost. The holdouts, almost a thousand men, women and children, had fled to Masada, according to accounts by a historian named Josephus, and survived there for three years.

"Archeologists are still excavating the site," Benjamin said as we waited in line for a cable car. "They disagree about whether the events happened as Josephus described them."

Normally, I place my trust in scientific research. My current quest made archeology irrelevant. "Which version would Lydia have heard?" I asked. "Your best guess."

"The traditional one."

"Let's hear it."

We started forward with a small group. "As soon as we're on the site," Benjamin said.

Carried higher and higher above the desert floor in our cable car, I focused on the flat-topped mountain ahead. Early-morning light cast the western slope into shadows and heightened the reflective glare of the tumbled stone ruins. For the desperate Jews who'd taken refuge here, it must have shone with hope, until the Romans laid siege.

We emerged onto a flat expanse marked by ruins. Benjamin identified a temple, barracks and other structures, including dovecotes. Doves, he explained, were kosher to eat.

"Do you know where she fell?" I asked.

"I'm sorry, no." He didn't have to inquire who I meant.

Two young women approached, holding cell phones. They spoke to us in German, then English. Take their pictures? Yes, of course.

I wielded one, my guide the other. Smiles, thanks, and, after a brief pause, off they went.

"They were flirting," Benjamin said.

"With us?"

"With who else?"

"Flirting with an obsessed widower and a gay man. That's like fishing in the Dead Sea." I'd become comfortable enough with my guide to blurt what was on my mind.

He resumed his narration. A Roman legion, unable to reach the rebels, had brought Jewish slaves from the Galilee to haul tons of earth and rocks for a ramp.

"The people of Masada also came from Galilee," Benjamin observed as he escorted me around low stone walls that defined ancient rooms. "The slaves may have included friends or relatives. The rebels refused to harm them by pouring boiling water or oil."

"Clever Romans." Clever in their cruelty.

Rather than be enslaved, torn from their families and forced to worship Roman gods, the holdouts chose to die. Suicide being a sin against God, the men had killed their own families, then drawn lots to choose who among them would slay the others. In the end, only one man had to kill himself.

"The story is that an old woman hid her grandchildren.

When the conquerors arrived at this gruesome scene of nearly a thousand dead bodies, it was she who related what had happened," Benjamin said.

I'd heard enough for now. "I need to be alone." With the sunlight intensifying and the number of visitors swelling, that would soon be impossible.

"Text me when you're ready." He headed toward a patch of shade and a wall low enough to sit on.

Stepping cautiously on the uneven surface, I went to a viewing area at the cliff's edge. In the gaps between stone walls, a metal fence reached waist-high.

As a knot of tourists moved off, I stared into the abyss. If Lydia had fallen here, it hadn't been by chance. Simply not feasible. Nor, I guessed, had she died at this spot by intention, because when I leaned over, I calculated that a leaper might hit an outcropping and suffer less than fatal damage. Unlikely that she'd have risked that.

There were other observation spots, some protected only by medium-height stone walls. Nearing one, I paused at the sight of a small woman, dark hair whipping in the breeze, staring down at the desert. She fingered a thin chain around her throat.

For my wife's thirtieth birthday, I'd commissioned a necklace of gold and silver to weave together the strands of her identity. The pendant had been her birthstone, a blue-green opal with hidden depths.

She'd left it at home when she flew to Israel. Because it was risky to travel with jewelry? Or because she'd been distancing herself from me symbolically as well as physically?

Or maybe she'd intended to die here, and hadn't wanted to leave it in the desert. Trying again, in a convoluted way, to protected me.

When the woman swung around, she bore little

resemblance to Lydia, aside from height and hair color. The pendant was a Hebrew letter I'd heard referred to as a *Chai*, which meant Life.

Once she left, I walked to the stone barrier. Below, the cliff fell away in a sheer drop. The impression strengthened, that my wife had stood here.

The wind picked up. Whispering. Wailing. Whipping my thoughts around, shrouding me in Lydia's despair, in her grandparents' tragedies, in the memories of murdered children who were now only starlike glimmers in a make-believe sky. I heard the weeping of people who had watched death approach as the ramp grew day by day.

Lydia and I overlapped. I felt her hand touching her throat, seeking but not finding the opal. At the final moment, unable to touch our years together, our love.

With a stab, I understood the pain that had propelled her to leap. I wished she'd let me join her and hold her in my arms, so we could have gone over the damn cliff together.

*"Promise you'll come back, Eric."*

Was this what Tory had feared? That, like Lydia, I would seek the infinite relief of abandoning the fight?

But I had a purpose beyond myself. To be there for others. To go where I was meant to go, and that was not over a cliff.

Tears coursed down my face.

Maybe I did believe in God, after all.

# CHAPTER EIGHTEEN

"How r u?" Tory texted when I informed her, digitally, that we were en route to Ben Gurion Airport.

"Still processing," I texted back, and soon fell asleep in the car beside Benjamin.

During sleep, researchers say, our brains take out the mental garbage. They tidy up, organize, and integrate memories and experiences. I suppose mine must have performed those functions intermittently during the next uncounted hours, as I said goodbye to my guide and endured the annoyance of airport security, two flights with a long layover in between, and fellow passengers who got up and down when I longed to sleep, and slept when I longed to get up and down.

I arrived in Los Angeles feeling like Gumby the stretchy cartoon character popular among my patients' children, right down to the green color. Collecting my bag of dirty laundry, I stumbled through Customs, navigated the chaos of people cluttering the curb, and caught a cab. Tory hadn't been able to meet me, nor did I expect her to.

After a brief attempt at conversation, the driver resumed listening to a game on the radio in an unfamiliar language.

According to my phone and the fading winter sun, it was afternoon in California, which meant the middle of the night in Israel. Recalling my strategy about staying awake on local time, I defied my instincts and clung to wakefulness.

On my cul-de-sac, the three-story house rose solemnly, its pale-gray brickwork and dark half-timbering offering little warmth. The only bright spots were the pink camellias abloom in front and, at the curb, Keith's red sports car.

Not his police-issue black vehicle. Was he taking a break? Why here?

Hoping there wasn't bad news waiting inside, I paid, tipped the driver, and carted my bag into the entry. Ahead, the staircase curved upward, while a rosy glow through the skylight suffused the hall. Whatever ghosts lingered had faded into columns of dust motes.

"Eric!" My sister-in-law's voice raced ahead of her. Skidding a little in her stocking feet, she plunged at me, all five-feet-ten-inches of her, and we nearly collapsed onto the polished stone floor. Only a quick bracing on my part held us upright.

"Don't kill the man. Not till he tells us what he's discovered, anyway." Keith paced in her wake, wearing his shoes and a business suit. If he was off duty, it barely showed.

"What brings you here?" I asked him.

"Tory's been freaking out," he said.

"Like you haven't?" she demanded.

Fear lurched in my chest. "The BRCA test?" Damn. I'd mentally set it aside.

"I'm clear." Tory released me with a squeeze of the shoulders. "It was negative."

"Good news." Fantastic, in fact. Picking up my bag, I eyed the staircase. It loomed as high as Masada. "I should sit down for a minute."

"In here." Keith indicated the great room.

A strange sort of circle closed around me as I dropped into an armchair, facing Keith and Tory. Two and a half years ago, they'd appeared at my door with the devastating news of Lydia's death. Now here they were, expecting some sort of closure. I wasn't sure I had any.

Tory curled on the couch, feet against Keith's leg. "Are you handling this okay?" he asked me.

That was an unusual question for my old buddy. "You're worried about me?"

"Last time, you fell down the stairs." So he'd been remembering that day, too.

"Just tired," I said. "You sure you care to listen to this? It's not as if I uncovered any major secrets."

"Yes. And I'm tired too," he growled. "The media's stirring things up and the chief's pushing for a resolution, not to mention I have other cases. This is a short break. Don't waste it."

"Fair enough." I recited the past few days' events, starting with the shock of seeing Chava, my Lydia from an alternate dimension. Then the grandparents' trauma and deaths when the boys were babies.

"When I think of grandparents, I picture old people," Tory said.

"They weren't old." I wasn't sure of their ages. "In their thirties, I guess."

"They probably looked old," Keith said. "Considering they'd gone through hell."

I recalled Chava's description of their photograph. "That sounds right." My account continued with the brothers' argument and the estrangement that lasted for the rest of their lives. Abruptly, I recalled another item. "According to Chava, one of the reasons Lydia hesitated to share her diagnosis with me was because of my father."

"What about your father?" Tory asked.

"He felt responsible for not insisting my mother get mammograms. Lydia figured I'd blame myself about her condition, too."

"Like you don't blame yourself anyway?" Tory flared.

"That's pretty much what Chava said. And a lot more, most of it negative. She and Lydia must have had a rather prickly conversation."

"How's that?" Keith began massaging Tory's feet.

Might as well share the rest. "She considered Lydia weak. The product of an indulgent society where people aren't in a constant struggle for survival."

"She might be surprised," Keith muttered.

I had to agree. Police officers, firefighters, doctors, nurses— some of us witness darkness on a daily basis. "I'm just relaying her perspective."

"That's it?" he said. "All you got from Lydia's cousin?"

"Basically, yes."

"What happened at Masada?" Tory prompted.

"*Could* she have fallen by accident?" Keith added.

As I filled them in about the clifftop refuge and the stark drop into the Judean desert, my voice cracked. Part of me remained there. And part of Masada, dust and rocks and despair, had stayed with me.

"You could faint or slip, especially if you were foolish, taking a selfie on top of a wall, for instance," I said. "But I think the authorities got it wrong, about her falling by accident."

My small audience sat in silence. Out of questions, as I was out of answers.

Time to move on. "Learn anything from the bartender?" I presumed that, despite her skepticism, Tory had heeded Benjamin's suggestion.

No reaction from Keith. He'd obviously heard the story.

"I went to see him yesterday," she said. "He claimed he already told us everything."

"Did you mention that an Israeli tour guide believes he's lying?"

"Yeah, that would go over big." Keith's hand strayed up Tory's leg. She didn't object. "The antagonize-the-witness school of interrogation."

"I mentioned that I understand being discreet," Tory said. "But, if he's interfering with a police investigation, it could cost him his bartending license."

"How'd he react?" Keith asked.

"He promised to think about it."

"Which means there's something to think about," he noted.

"Yes!" I nodded for emphasis.

They regarded me with question marks.

"We're missing a point. Not necessarily involving the bartender, but ..." I struggled to identify the uneasiness running through me.

"Are we still discussing my sister?" Tory asked uncertainly.

"No, Alison. Perhaps both."

Keith tilted his head. "What are you implying?"

"Don't interrupt while I'm thinking." I'd nearly lost the thread. How irritating. "A woman with a suspicious lump tests positive for the BRCA mutation and refuses a biopsy. It never occurred to Alison that she might be suicidal? Why didn't she counsel Lydia?"

Keith's mouth twisted in discontent. Not what he'd been looking for.

"Maybe she did offer counsel," Tory said. "My sister was good at ignoring what she didn't want to hear."

"Or Alison was too caught up in her own drama, her unresolved crap." I waved my hand, dismissing my word choice. "Rape isn't crap. But it created a screen between her and her patients. If this had been my case, if a woman declined a biopsy, I'd have urged her to bring in her husband or partner. I'd have pressed her to discuss the matter with them and me."

"Is this going anywhere?" Keith asked.

Yes, into anger—at my dead colleague. "Lydia's cousin believes she was a coward for not fighting for her life. Well, if Alison's trauma interfered with her ability to fulfill her duty to her patients, why didn't *she* fight it? Or did she, and we haven't yet discovered how? It might be a clue we've overlooked."

"You mean her motive for going to Dr. Radman's house the night she died?" Tory prompted.

"Right. Or..." The problem with thinking out loud is that, when you run out of steam, you have an audience expecting more. And that was as far as I'd gotten.

Tory's phone sounded. *Saved by the bell.*

She glanced at the screen. Angled it away from Keith. "Gotta take this." Scrambled to her feet and strolled off.

Alone with my friend, I asked, "You guys back together?"

"Excuse me, what?"

"The foot rubbing business."

He snorted. "Can we skip the girl talk? Long story short, could have been a scary diagnosis, so I stuck around, but it wasn't. What's your theory about Dr. Abrams?"

"I'm working on that."

"Turn on the news!" Tory yelled. "Hurry!"

While Keith fiddled with his phone, I grabbed the remote and clicked on the large- screen TV. A swift change of channels brought us to Hayden O'Donnell, square-faced and solemn, wielding his mic in front of a stone wall that fronted a large, modern house.

"We'll replay that video in a minute." Behind the reporter, a uniformed officer struggled to corral a bunch of milling protesters. Their waving and contradictory signs—"Lock up rapists!" vs. "It's a frame job!"—appeared in imminent danger of stabbing each other. "If you're just tuning in, I'm at the home of celebrity psychiatrist Ward Radman, where, minutes ago, shots were fired."

"Oh, hell." Keith leaped up. Simultaneously, his phone buzzed. "How does she get tipped off before I do?"

"It isn't a contest," Tory said.

But, of course, it was.

My detective friend strode out while Tory and I watched the screen. In a replay, O'Donnell was interviewing Brandy Cornello, her short dark hair rumpled and her mouth pressed into a hard line.

"Ms. Cornello," he intoned. "Since you discovered Dr. Abrams' body and have been accused of moving her car..."

"I haven't been accused of anything except by irresponsible members of the media." The nurse wore a uniform-style pantsuit, as if she'd arrived from the office.

"Look behind her." Tory indicated a young Hispanic woman scowling at the camera. "She's familiar."

Her sign read "Radman=Rapist." "Is she the woman you hauled in for defacing the wall?" I hazarded.

"That's it! Kit Sanchez," Tory confirmed.

"I stand corrected," the reporter was saying to Nurse Cornello. "But as a witness, isn't it a conflict of interest to participate in a protest?"

Brandy spread her hands. "I'm simply exercising my freedom of speech."

On the video, two sharp bangs aroused panicky screams and sent the demonstrators scurrying. O'Donnell cringed and Brandy ducked. "Did you hear that?" he asked the camera. "I believe those were gunshots."

Anxiously, the nurse glanced toward Kit. Why? Did they

know each other?

The clip ended. "That occurred a few minutes ago here at Dr. Ward Radman's house in Safe Harbor." O'Donnell swallowed before continuing. "We've had no reports of injuries. Police are pursuing a motorcyclist who left the scene." In response to someone off-camera, he added, "No, we don't think the motorcycle backfired. Police have recovered a bullet of unknown caliber. We'll update you as we learn more."

"Gotta go." Tory retrieved her purse.

I muted the news. "Who alerted you?"

She grinned. "Nat the bartender. He called to say he's up for a little chat. Just a bonus that the TV was on in the bar and he started yelling about it."

She might have to share any information she gleaned from Nat, but it was a victory of sorts. Again, she'd beaten Keith to the punch.

"Good luck." Curious as I was about Nat and Alison, I was in no mood to tag along. Not that Tory would have allowed it.

After she left, I remained in the armchair, wondering whether I would ever be able to move again. Well, I had promised to resume work the next day. But did I really have to lug my suitcase upstairs and fall into bed? I could sleep here.

Then something happened that roused me to my feet. My father-in-law arrived home, and I smelled dinner.

# CHAPTER NINETEEN

Despite the temptation to sit by myself and doze over lunch on Thursday, I joined Rod and Jeremiah in the cafeteria. "Maybe it's bad luck for us to sit together," I remarked.

"Why is that?" Jeremiah asked.

"The last time we shared a table was exactly a week ago," I said. "And a bomb went off. We meet again, right after shots are fired."

"That is not logical." He removed a frilly toothpick from atop his sandwich. "One thing is not related to the other."

"Must be the caffeine talking." I'd compensated for time-shifted weariness by overdosing on coffee.

"What baffles me," Rod muttered over his burrito, "is why people keep acting as if Jer is responsible for that guy's problems." He cast an annoyed glance at a staffer strutting by in his OnWard, UpWard T-shirt. The anesthesiologist had replaced his habitual mocking of our companion with a protective attitude.

"People want to lay blame somewhere," I pointed out.

The latest developments were frustrating. The motorcyclist had evaded capture, and the media demanded results. These days, the public expected forensic evidence, such as the recovered bullet, to lead instantly to an arrest.

In his latest radio broadcast, Ward had harped on the theme that he was the victim of a conspiracy. Although he didn't cite anyone specifically, murmurs and sneers about my tablemate persisted among a handful of staff members.

"It is ironic that they would suspect me of attacking him," Jeremiah said. "I do not own a gun."

"If you did, who would you shoot first?" Rod asked.

Jeremiah puzzled over this. "Must people be shot in order?"

The anesthesiologist didn't hesitate. "Ward would top my list."

"That reminds me. I have a different kind of list." Our solemn friend proceeded to hand us each a computer-printed flier. "You are invited on Saturday."

Rod dug out his reading glasses. "What's a move-in party?"

"I estimate the movers will have relocated my furniture to my new home by 3 p.m.," Jeremiah responded. "We will celebrate that I have escaped the watchful eye of Mrs. Linden."

Rod tugged his short beard. "I'm afraid my wife has other plans." He didn't specify what.

Conjuring an excuse would take my jet-lagged brain a minute. Stalling, I said, "I thought you didn't mind her snooping."

"She exceeded reasonable boundaries," he replied. "Fortunately, I had not paid my March rent. I have also invited former co-workers and your sister-in-law, Eric."

"Why Tory?"

"She brought excellent food to my apartment," he reminded me. "I have ordered the same from your father-in-law for this occasion."

"Including eyeballs in the popcorn?" I couldn't resist asking.

"There'll be eyeballs in the popcorn?" Judging by Rod's

reaction, he was regretting his refusal.

"I told her they were optional," Jeremiah said.

I had no idea whether Tory would accept, aside from dropping off the food as a favor to her dad. However, Jeremiah's former colleagues from Alison's office might have useful insights. I'd be sure to text her about the guest list.

Thus far, her investigation had yielded tantalizing but inconclusive results. The bartender had admitted hearing Alison talk to a man at the bar about using ketamine to treat a friend's PTSD. Since he'd missed parts of the conversation, however, Nat couldn't swear that she'd sought to buy the drug, and he claimed he didn't recognize her companion. He hadn't spoken up sooner, he'd said, because it would damage his business if police caught someone selling drugs there.

Although she'd shared this information with Keith, Tory planned to seek additional witnesses on her own. I'd texted Benjamin about the upshot of his tip, and received a smiling emoji.

"I would appreciate if you would attend, Eric," Jeremiah broke into my reflections. "I could use your assistance in positioning my furnishings."

When I scanned the invitation again, the address struck me as familiar. "You're moving into Alison's house?"

"Seriously?" Rod studied his printed sheet. "How is that possible?"

"Celia heard other nurses discussing a cheap rental opportunity," Jeremiah said. "They think that, because a person died in the house, tenants would not wish to live there. Brandy did not require a deposit, since she knows me."

"Isn't the estate in probate?" I asked.

"Her attorney has assured her that, in California, the executor has the authority to rent property immediately," Jeremiah replied.

"You don't mind about Alison's body being found in the tub?" Rod appeared genuinely unsettled.

"I am not superstitious," Jeremiah said.

Housewarmings aren't my favorite way to spend a Saturday, nor was I eager to revisit the site of Alison's demise. Yet, Jeremiah had been Alison's lover, and Brandy her nurse. Her old partner, Chuck, might attend, along with other colleagues. Might there be a reason of the cosmic variety summoning me to this gathering?

"Also, I hope on Saturday you will tell me what you have learned about Lydia," Jeremiah added.

Lydia, who'd been Alison's patient. Not that I was superstitious, either, but... "I wouldn't miss it," I said.

\*

Alison's possessions had been removed and Jeremiah's belongings deposited before the guests arrived. His sagging sofa and worn chairs fit comfortably in the living room, where Brandy had neither replaced the carpeting nor repainted.

To me, the house seemed to grieve for its former owner. On the walls, dark rectangles marked where photos of babies and mothers had hung. In the kitchen, the chipped counter—stripped of its boxes, cans and appliances—had a forlorn air.

Several women, co-workers I'd met at the funeral, brought dishware, glasses, and other items as gifts. They applied themselves to stowing these in cabinets and drawers, while avoiding any discussion of Alison's death. As for Tory, after arriving with the food, she applied her skills to setting up the TV and WiFi. And eavesdropping, I presumed.

Chuck stayed in his former partner's home only a short while, growing increasingly uneasy. When he peeked into the bathroom, he blanched. Doctors tend to develop strong stomachs, but that doesn't necessarily apply when a person close to us is involved. After mumbling an excuse about his daughter's soccer game, he departed.

"It is strange, is it not?" Jeremiah remarked as he and I adjusted the placement of his double bed. "She and I had intercourse on this mattress, and now it occupies her room."

"Right." More than strange, in my view. Downright creepy.

"I still do not understand why she chose me." Even when my rangy friend straightened to his full height, he merged with the modest room rather than dominating it. "I do believe she enjoyed herself. I think she would be glad that I am the person living in her space."

"We can't know what the dead would think, can we?" Certainly, I couldn't.

At Jeremiah's request, I proceeded to outline my experiences in Israel. He said little, except, "I wish I had a cousin who could explain about my grandparents. They never discussed how they survived the Holocaust or reached New York, where they met."

"They never talked about it at all?" What a devastating past to hold inside.

"They were so eager for my mother to feel normal that they pretended there were relatives in England, and gave her gifts and letters from them on her birthday," he said. "Later, she noticed that the letters were in her mother's handwriting, and that there were no envelopes with foreign postmarks. After my grandmother died, my grandfather admitted it had been a ruse."

Finished with the bedroom, he and I prowled into the kitchen, where Brandy was removing a tray of mini-pizzas from the oven. "I figured these would taste better warmed up," she said.

Tory had set out snacks on the counter. As promised, they were much like those at the funeral, minus the eyeballs and pink-and-purple coloring. "Normally we bring hot trays," she said, joining us.

"I told your father it was not necessary," Jeremiah said.

"Regardless, that's my job." Snatching up potholders, Tory took the tray from the nurse, who held on for a second longer than necessary. Quite a contrast, those two: Tory the taller by half a foot, with reddish-brown hair to her shoulders; Brandy chocolate-skinned, with short dark curls and a hostile expression directed at my sister-in-law.

"Problem?" Tory had never been one to dodge an issue.

"I hear you're working to exonerate that bastard." Brandy's voice rang out, quieting other guests.

"It's my job to ferret out the truth and assist his attorney," Tory stated.

"You should be ashamed!"

Jeremiah maintained silence while plucking up a mini-pizza. I did the same.

"Saw you on TV," Tory remarked, seizing the opportunity to pounce on a potential source. "How do you know Kit Sanchez?"

"What makes you think I do?"

"For starters, just now, you didn't ask who she is." Tory lowered the tray to a hot pad. Another woman scooted forward to snatch an hors d'oeuvre. "And the pair of you exchanged glances after the shooting."

"I met her at the protest," Brandy answered. "She said Radman raped her sister. How do *you* know her?"

"I arrested her," Tory said. "Several years ago, for vandalism. She graffitied Dr. Radman's wall."

"I wish she'd done a lot worse to him!"

"A witness claims Dr. Abrams bought ketamine from a drug dealer," Tory said. "Did you know about that? If it's true, it could clear Radman in her death."

"How low can you sink?" Brandy's hands clenched. "You'd do anything for that creep, wouldn't you?"

"Same as I'd do for any client."

"Which shows what a scumbag you are!"

Tory didn't flinch. "Dr. Abrams claimed the ketamine was to treat someone's PTSD. Was it yours?"

"Like hell!"

"Hey, guys." A woman held up her phone. "The cops released a picture of the shooting suspect, the guy on the motorcycle."

Brandy hurried over. Tory fumbled irritably with her cell. "It's not working. Probably another damn update."

I shared mine, where a few taps took us to a helmetless biker scowling across his handlebars at the camera. The blurred image showed close-cropped hair, medium coloring, and sharp cheekbones.

"Facial recognition might identify him," a woman said.

"Well, if it had, they wouldn't need the public's help, would they?" Brandy grumbled.

My sister-in-law had gone silent. Her nostrils flared.

"What?" I said.

"None of your business." Snatching my phone, she stalked out of the room, and the house.

I followed. Otherwise, she was likely to drive off with my cell. As a doctor, I required it in case of emergency.

Phone to her ear, she skimmed from the porch down to the sidewalk. "Keith. Me. I know that guy."

Despite her glare, I approached close enough to listen. And to catch the part that explained her intensity.

"He's a handyman," she said. "He works for Ward Radman."

# CHAPTER TWENTY

The shooter, identified by several viewers as handyman Josiah Eckert, age forty-seven, was arrested on Sunday. Tory, the only witness to connect him to Radman, spent several hours at the police station recounting her tale of encountering him at her client's house a few weeks earlier. Confronted with her statement, Eckert admitted doing odd jobs for Radman.

His latest job had been odder than most.

"On the plus side, they haven't mentioned you on the news," I commented the next morning while, at the kitchen counter, my sister-in-law stared morosely at her laptop. "I presume you'd rather not be publicized for ratting out your client."

"Regardless, I had to notify his attorney, the one who recommended hiring me." She pushed a chunk of pancake around on her plate. "He understands I couldn't withhold evidence. But my prospects for remaining on this case are, shall we say, dim. I'd like to nail down that drug dealer before they kick me off."

Getting fired by Ward Radman wouldn't be the worst thing that ever happened, I mused. I didn't say so, mostly because I was attacking my breakfast with gusto.

Morris, who'd been piling surplus pancakes in a container,

gestured toward the newspaper I hadn't had a chance to read. "According to the *Journal*, this fellow Eckert insists it was a harmless prank. He aimed at the wall."

"A prank in exchange for a five-hundred-dollar deposit in his bank account?" Tory scoffed. "Not to mention that discharging a loaded gun near a crowd is far from harmless."

"He denies placing that bomb in Dr. Radman's car." Morris spoke with the rapt tone of a fan who's been binge-watching his favorite show.

"Doesn't matter," I said. It was Radman's connection to the shooting that counted. It implied he'd set up the fake attack to strengthen his claim of being victimized. This cast doubt—further doubt—an almost everything he alleged.

"Have you checked the *Journal's* website?" Morris asked his daughter. "There might be a new development."

"Dad! It's eight o'clock in the morning."

"That Montenegro woman is a real go-getter," he said. "Better than those L.A. reporters, if you ask me."

Tory indulged him by clicking to the site. She sighed. "You're right. She's interviewing Kit Sanchez."

"The nurse?" Tugging off the apron that covered his striped pajamas, Morris hurried to stand beside her.

"No, you're thinking of Brandy Cornello. Kit's the woman who accused him of raping her sister."

"Thanks. It's hard to keep track."

I joined them. My office hours didn't start until nine. Although I liked to arrive early, how could I miss this?

"You're saying Dr. Radman raped your sister but the police in Azalea Springs did nothing?" Smartly dressed in a tailored suit, Soraya leaned forward in her chair. She and her subject, a young woman whose baggy sweater matched her light-brown hair, were wedged into an alcove. There was a rack of tourist brochures behind them and, on the wall, a sign reading For

Long-Term Rates, See Manager.

"He lied and said Lourdes agreed to have sex with him." Kit trembled with anger. "Her fiancé believed him, called her a slut and broke it off. I found her hanging in our bedroom. The note said her heart was broken. She was twenty-two years old. That bastard did this and got away with it."

"I'm sorry." Soraya drew a deep breath. "How long ago was this?"

"Twelve years." A buzzer went off, the kind that indicates a customer's arrival. "Excuse me. I have to see about that."

As Kit hurried out of view, Tory jotted a note. "She must work at a motel."

To the audience, the reporter said, "This is Soraya Montenegro, talking with Kit Sanchez. She's been active in demonstrations against Dr. Ward Radman and... Oh, good, you're back."

"Just someone dropping off a key." Kit perched on her chair.

Rapid-fire, Soraya posed the next question. "What's your reaction to the news that Dr. Radman may have hired someone to shoot up his property?"

"I'm glad they caught the guy!" Loathing transformed her face into a vindictive mask. It occurred to me that this tragedy had not only cost Lourdes her life, but had consumed Kit's as well. "It shows what a fraud Radman is. He killed my sister and he killed Dr. Abrams. He has to pay!"

Soraya tensed. The next question must be explosive, I speculated. And it was. "A reliable source told me Dr. Abrams bought ketamine, the drug that killed her. Wouldn't that tend to exonerate Dr. Radman in her death?"

Kit's mouth fell open. She panted as if she'd just run a race.

"Nat didn't see Alison buy drugs," Tory muttered. "Either Soraya's exaggerating or there's a new witness."

"Or she misunderstood," Morris said. "Let's be fair."

I'd have gone with exaggerating.

Kit shook off her surprise. "Ward Radman is a liar and a rapist. He probably bribed your source, just like he bribed the gunman."

"It's a credible account," Soraya persisted.

"Who do you suppose is her source?" Morris was breathing down my neck. Or rather, since he's significantly shorter than me, I was breathing down his. "I'll bet it's Radman's attorney."

That was my bet, too.

"He can't escape justice again! I've waited too long for this." A phone rang in the background. "I have to go."

"Thank you, Kit Sanchez." Into the camera, Soraya identified herself again, and signed off.

"She's a sharp one," my father-in-law said.

Tory grimaced.

"So are you," Morris added.

"Thanks."

"You might ask where she shops," he said. "That suit's flattering."

Tory rolled her eyes. Not taking fashion advice from Dad, even if he was right.

Head buzzing with the latest Radman pros and cons, I drove to my office. I resented getting caught up in this soap opera. Also, I resented how much it fascinated me.

A pair of earplugs and a set of blinders like old-time hackney horses wore might have proved useful at work. It was hard to escape snatches of speculation among my nurse, Isaiah's nurse and the receptionist. Several of my patients updated the news on their phones during their exams, and one asked me point-blank if I knew Radman and if he was being framed.

I pleaded ignorance.

In the hospital cafeteria, the usual rumor-mongerers were

smirking, gloating, and sneering in Jeremiah's direction. Radman's latest audio, embroidering on the fact that he'd rented Alison's house, had implied that Jeremiah was deeply enmeshed in the entire scenario.

Across the cafeteria, dozens of phones beeped to announce a text. All at once? While not an emergency siren, this required attention.

"All available staff to the auditorium." The message had been sent by Mark Rayburn, our administrator. Normally, such gatherings are announced by the public relations director, with plenty of advance notice.

"Has Mark confided in you as to the purpose?" Jeremiah asked as we rose.

"Your guess is as good as mine," I said.

"Maybe they're selling the hospital to some nefarious conglomerate who'll put accountants in every operating room." Rod scratched beneath his colorful surgical cap. "Oh, wait. They already did that."

Despite the usual complaints about our owner, a hospital corporation in Kentucky, I would hardly term it nefarious. Still, I shared the anxious uncertainty that rippled through the staff as we moved, like a giant blood clot, to the designated gathering site.

The wood-paneled auditorium featured steeply raked tiers of comfortable seats. It filled quickly, with standing room at the back.

The powerful figure of the administrator commanded the stage, his stance a reminder that he'd played football in high school. Although normally affable, he was scowling.

When the shuffling and rustling abated, he spoke into the mic. "You're busy people, so I'll get to the point. We are all concerned about the recent death of our colleague, Dr. Alison Abrams, and a certain level of curiosity is understandable.

What disturbs me is that some staff members are smearing the reputation of one of our doctors based on innuendo and gossip.

"This unprofessional behavior must cease. In addition, I expect each and every person who has insulted this doctor to apologize to him, in person or in writing. That's it. Any questions?"

Beside me, Rod raised his hand.

The corners of Mark's mouth twitched. "Yes, Rod?"

"To expedite matters, I'd like to suggest you post a groveling box in the cafeteria where offenders can place their apologies," he said.

A chuckle ran through the room.

Paige Brennan added in a ringing tone, "I wouldn't mind if we read them aloud, since most of us have had to witness this offensive conduct."

Other voices agreed. Jeremiah blinked in what I took to be astonishment that so many colleagues were on his side.

Mark raised a hand for quiet. "While I share your frustration, there will be no shaming. Apologies may be presented in private. Thank you for listening."

As we rose to file out, Jeremiah said to Rod, "I do not believe a groveling box is necessary."

"Wouldn't hurt, though."

In the aisle, several people approached him, muttering phrases like, "Sorry if I offended."

"There's a kiss-your-sister apology," commented my brother-in-law, Barry, stuck behind us in the slow-moving queue.

"What does that mean?" I asked.

"No passion in it." He shot me a grin.

The mood among my friends bordered on cheerful, approaching jubilant. It felt as if we'd won a round. But, to me, the victory rang hollow.

A ghost drifted among us, her features fading too quickly. With the emphasis on scandal and cross-accusations, on who had bombed Radman's car and whether Alison had bought the drugs that took her life, she as a person had nearly vanished from the picture.

As I headed to the medical building, I pictured her walking beside me. Her long-legged stride matched mine; she wore her light-brown hair skinned back; her tense jaw reflected stress.

How many times had she been betrayed? By her predator of a soccer coach, by the medical school mentor who'd raped her, by a culture that told women to suck it up if they expected to succeed in what had once been termed "a man's world." When my mother had mentioned that phrase to me, I'd shrugged it off as a Victorian relic. Even sympathetic guys like me hadn't understood how badly women's lives were being warped.

It was unfair for Alison's memory to be overshadowed by the circumstances surrounding her death. Mostly, I hated that, whether she'd died by accident or by design, she hadn't fought back.

At the funeral, her brother had quoted a commandment to help our loved ones to their rest. Although I hadn't been among Alison's loved ones, someone ought to care enough not to let her voice shrivel into a mere sound bite.

By the end of the day, I'd suppressed those thoughts. Until the sight of a silver luxury car in front of my house brought them rushing back.

It wasn't Radman's convertible—that was presumably held as evidence after the bombing—but a second car I'd seen on the news. Its personalized plate had been evident as it rolled into his gated driveway, narrowly avoiding protesters. He must have driven here to fire Tory in person for identifying the shooter.

A red fury nearly blinded me. I had to sit in the garage for several minutes to regain control.

But what if the monster inside was attacking her? That notion shot me out of the car and through the door.

Smell of coffee. Low murmur of voices. Two figures to my left: Tory standing with her laptop open on the kitchen side of the counter, and, across from her, a gaunt man wearing Ward Radman's expensive suit. He occupied a stool, both hands cupping a coffee mug like a bum absorbing its warmth.

In a little over two weeks, the man had lost as much weight as a cancer patient, an impression amplified by his hunched posture. On his cheek throbbed a red scar from the bomb blast. As I drew closer, I noted traces of makeup smeared unevenly over the gray skin on his face and neck, to ghoulish effect.

My brain ticked off possible medical causes, including severe PTSD. But while Radman had suffered damage to his career and might be hit with criminal charges, men with egos less robust than his had survived worse. And profited from it.

As my sister-in-law acknowledged my presence, I prepared for the man's usual bluster. Instead, he peered at me blankly.

"Does it help if I admit I've been stupid?" he asked Tory.

"Stupid about what?" I prowled toward them. "Or should I say which?"

"Eric." Tory wasn't warning me off. Cautioning me, rather.

"I haven't been able to think straight." The psychiatrist shook his head. "I didn't bomb my car, but that gave me the idea. A few gunshots—I thought it would remind people I'm being framed."

"Remind?" I growled. "You mean fool them."

Radman continued addressing Tory. "Like I said, I'll double what I've been paying you. Triple it. You have to identify the man who sold Alison the ketamine."

Since Tory had insisted that was her goal, I anticipated a

quick assent. Instead, she replied, "You told your attorney I'm incompetent. That he should have my PI license revoked."

"That was before he explained it was you who persuaded the bartender to talk." Those owlish eyes had a dim cast, the mouth a desperate quaver. "You're the only person who can clear me."

She scanned her laptop screen. From my angle, I could see she was watching a cat video. "The police are hunting for the drug dealer."

"Not very hard!" he squawked. "Since I pulled that stupid business with the gunshots, everyone's writing me off. They're dismissing the fact that somebody, and we can all guess who, moved Alison's car to implicate me."

"Whatever Nurse Cornello might have done after the fact doesn't change what happened to Dr. Abrams," Tory said doggedly.

My sister-in-law had had enough, I gathered. Threats to impugn her reputation and have her license revoked had shattered whatever loyalty she'd felt. Good.

"Please. I need you. I'll pay whatever you want." Having run out of leverage, Ward was begging. I couldn't enjoy his defeat, however. It didn't undo the harm he'd caused a number of women. Nor did I trust this humility to last.

"No," Tory said.

A nervous tic jumped in his cheek. Perspiration stood out against the makeup.

For a moment, I thought he was working up an argument. Then, shoulders slumping, Ward Radman got to his feet and stumbled out of my house.

And, as it turned out, into thin air.

# CHAPTER TWENTY-ONE

Radman's disappearance was discovered about an hour and a half later by none other than Soraya Montenegro. I wouldn't have learned about it for another half hour, until I received an unexpected visitor, if not for Morris.

He insisted that, in exchange for his surplus meals, Tory set up her laptop on the table so we could watch Soraya's live videocast. "Dr. Radman promised her an interview at his house," Morris filled us in, having listened to the audio version in his van. "We can't miss this!"

Tory contacted Radman's attorney to be sure he was aware of the situation. "He's driving over there now," she said. "Talk about acting stupid! I can't believe a murder suspect is conducting an interview with the press."

"I hope he doesn't lawyer up." My father-in-law, who had claimed the seat with the best view, drew upon his vast store of legal terminology from cop shows. "The public has a right to know."

"Actually, not," his daughter said.

I shrugged. I have a policy against talking with a full mouth. Also, I was hoping Ward Radman would basically screw himself.

Soraya had parked in the driveway behind the car with the personalized plate that had very recently graced my curb. Although she often recorded her own video, she had brought a camera operator, to whom she spoke in animated fashion. She proceeded up a flagstone walkway along the front of the one-story house, at major risk to her ankles, since she wore her customary sky-high heels and a red dress.

"I'm excited for this opportunity to talk in person with celebrity psychiatrist Ward Radman," she gushed. "Isn't this a beautiful house, overlooking the ocean here in Safe Harbor, California!"

The reference to the location, in what I considered a local story, was a reminder of the international interest. Was Benjamin watching? Quick calculation: it must be about five-thirty a.m. in Israel.

Soraya pressed the bell. Inside, chimes played the opening notes of "Over the Rainbow."

No response.

She tried again. Again, only the melody.

The reporter and her camera operator ventured around the property. In the back sprawled a pool and deck on several levels, with a spectacular view of the harbor's twinkling lights far below. "Hello?" she ventured. "Anyone home? Dr. Radman?"

No answer.

"Surely there's staff," Morris commented.

"The housekeeper doesn't live on the premises," Tory said.

The rear of the house was mostly glass. There seemed to be lights on inside, but due to tinting, we couldn't see in.

"Where is he?" Morris clasped his hands atop the table.

I got a bad feeling. "Surely he wasn't that desperate."

"Don't go there," Tory said.

"What do you mean?" her father asked.

We were spared the need to answer when Soraya slid open

the rear patio door. "It isn't locked," she told viewers, unnecessarily. "Since he did invite me, I suppose it's okay to go in."

"No, it isn't." Tory was texting. "Keith ought to be aware of this. If it's a crime scene, she's about to contaminate it."

"A crime scene?" Morris was vibrating hard, transfixed by the nosy reporter.

Were we about to see a dead body? Showing one on a live videocast would not only violate the deceased's privacy, it could traumatize children. Assuming their parents weren't already traumatizing them by letting them watch this drivel.

Soraya poked into a vast lounge-type room, where the camera swept the tasteful, low-key furnishings. No books or magazines, no personal pictures. Did an actual human live there?

At an inner doorway, Soraya hesitated. "Maybe he's taking a nap."

"Maybe he's dead," Tory grumbled.

"Why do you say that?" her father asked.

"Just a hunch."

The camera scanned a catering-size kitchen, where a cell phone lay on the counter. "He wouldn't leave without his phone!" Soraya trumpeted.

"Unless he has more than one," commented a man's voice, off-camera. The operator, I presumed.

"But his car's in the driveway." She shifted from one foot to the other. "I can't in good conscience leave without making sure he's all right."

Was this genuine concern? I recalled that, the previous year, one of her sources had been murdered after the killer learned she'd been spilling secrets to Soraya.

"Maybe it's like when Geraldo Rivera opened Al Capone's vault on live TV," my father-in-law opined. "Anybody remember that?"

We didn't. While the reporter prowled through a series of unoccupied rooms, he explained how a vault beneath a hotel once owned by the mafia boss had been opened, in a much-hyped telecast, to reveal only debris.

Ward Radman's house contained no debris. Nor did it contain Ward Radman.

"Gosh, this is strange." Her dark hair frizzing more than usual, Soraya faced us. "I'd better notify the police."

"Way ahead of you," Tory muttered.

As the reporter placed the call, the video captured every hem and haw and awkward response about who she was and why she was there. Although I presumed the attorney and Keith would arrive momentarily, time stretched as our self-appointed hostess wandered out to the front porch.

She filled the gap with speculation, and occasional reminders that we were at the Safe Harbor home of controversial psychiatrist etc. etc.

"Why would he invite me for an interview and then leave?" she asked rhetorically. "Is this a ploy to generate more publicity?"

"Good guess," Morris said.

"Yes, but whose ploy?" Tory asked. "We have only her word that he invited her in the first place."

Her father shook his head. "What makes you such a cynic?"

"Experience."

I shared her skepticism.

"Is it possible someone abducted him?" Soraya spoke breathlessly. "I didn't see signs of violence. Did you?"

Off-camera: "Nope."

"Why would someone kidnap Dr. Radman?" Having voiced this theory, she ran with it. "Where would they take him? What could they hope to accomplish? Oh, here's the police!"

A uniformed patrolman approached from the driveway, followed a minute later by my tall, blond friend. Sharply, Keith requested the cameraman shut off the video, and the viewing panel went black.

"I'll bet they can track him by his credit cards." Morris stared at the laptop as if the show might resume.

"If they have his credit info," Tory said.

"And he's only been missing a short time," my father-in-law noted. "Might not have charged anything yet."

"If he hired a car service, there'd be a record of where he went," I said, and immediately regretted participating in such an idiotic conversation.

The doorbell chimed.

Tory and I shot glances at each other. *Is that him?*

Reaching the door with my sister-in-law on my heels, I switched on the porch light. In the unflattering circle of light stood Alison's nurse, her wide-cheeked face creased with worry.

Great. The entire world had my address and felt free to use it.

"Miss Cornello," I said.

"Excuse me, Dr. Darcy." She peered anxiously at Tory. "Are you still working for Radman?"

"No."

"But you can locate him, right?" she pressed. "Don't you people put trackers in phones or something? Oh, darn. He doesn't have his phone, does he?" She must have been watching the same video.

I let her in. "What's this about?"

Brandy hugged herself protectively. Standing in the high-ceilinged entryway, close to Tory, she appeared even smaller than usual. "Detective Golden, I'm aware we didn't hit it off at our last meeting."

"Water under the bridge," Tory said. "What's up?"

From inside the house, noises marked my father-in-law's retreat to his bedroom. He must have listened long enough to ascertain that he hadn't won a front-row seat to Radman's latest antics. Aside from such obsessions, he tended to respect Tory's and my privacy.

Brandy swallowed. "Since you aren't working for Radman, I'll hire you."

"Even though I'm a—what did you call me—a scumbag?" Tory asked.

"I thought that was water under the bridge."

"Muddy water," my sister-in-law said. "Pray continue."

"If you work for me, you're bound by detective-client privilege, right?" Brandy said. "Nothing I tell you goes any further?"

"Doesn't apply to private investigators." Tory stood rock solid. "What did you plan to hire me for?"

Brandy's gaze traveled between her and me. "Look, I'd just as soon that bastard got what's coming to him. But if this is Kit's doing, she'll wreck her life. He deserves to go to prison. She doesn't."

I pictured the furious young woman who'd declared on camera that morning that Ward had to pay for her sister's and Alison's deaths. "You believe Kit kidnapped him?" I asked.

"Why?" Tory put in.

Brandy ducked her head. "This afternoon, she cornered me at the office. I had to get her out of there. She was disturbing the patients. She insisted I tell her if it was true what the reporter claimed, that Alison bought ketamine from a drug dealer. I... I had to confirm it. It never occurred to me she'd go ballistic."

"You knew Alison bought the drugs that killed her?" I asked.

"It was never supposed to work this way!" Brandy wailed.

"This whole business is like a runaway train."

My sister-in-law summarized the situation. "Kit believes he'll get off, so you think she's taking the law into her own hands. If she plans to kill him, why not do it at his house?"

"I don't know," Brandy said. "For six years, I've hated that monster. When Dr. Abrams told me he'd raped her, too, I couldn't see anything beyond revenge. It never occurred to me... we figured... Just find them and I'll explain everything. Please!"

"Have you told the police what you suspect?" Tory asked.

"No." Brandy's dark eyes widened. "Do we have to? It's only a suspicion. There's no proof. And you work for me!"

"Actually, I don't." Tory took out her phone. "Did Ms. Sanchez issue any direct threats toward Dr. Radman?"

"No. But..." A meaningful pause.

"But?" I demanded.

"She admitted to bombing his car, to scare him." Brandy rolled her eyes. "The woman's not behaving rationally."

"If she's the bomber, the police need that information." Tory pressed a number and got Keith. After a rapid-fire exchange, she clicked off. "He's busy at Radman's house. Said to keep him posted."

Brandy must have used the time to reflect. "What's your hourly rate?"

"Don't worry about it," Tory said. "Where does Ms. Sanchez live?"

"No idea."

"What about the motel?" I said. "She manages one, right?"

Brandy nodded. "The, uh, Safe and Sound."

"Swift and Snug. It's right by the freeway. I'm pretty sure I recognized it from when I was on patrol," Tory said. "It's a place to start."

While she texted our destination to Keith, I retrieved our

coats from the hall closet. Male ego or not, I wasn't letting Tory and Brandy go there alone.

# CHAPTER TWENTY-TWO

To my frustration, Tory ordered Brandy to avoid further discussion of Alison, the drugs and the whole revenge business. "Save it for the police," she said. "Unless it's relevant to what we're about to face, we can't risk corrupting your memory."

For once, I wished my sister-in-law weren't so damn conscientious. Why had Alison gone to Ward's house that fatal night? From what her nurse had blurted, I gathered she might have intended to fight back, finally. How, and what had gone wrong?

The radio crackled with news about Ward Radman's disappearance. Already, the announcer declared, there'd been numerous tips and sightings. Nothing had paid off, thus far.

The Swift & Snug Motel proved to be a two-story, L-shaped structure. As Tory parked between a car with Arizona plates and a dusty SUV, she indicated the attached coffee shop.

"We used to call that the Grift & Grub," she shouted above the rumble of the nearby freeway. "The coffee's so-so but the strawberry pie's fine." I wondered how anyone could taste it over the exhaust fumes.

Inside a small office familiar from Soraya's videocast, a young man sat behind the desk, tapping intently on his phone.

"Kit Sanchez here?" Tory asked.

He kept his eyes on the screen. "She's off tonight."

"Does she live on the premises?"

"Not officially."

"Where does she sleep, not officially?"

Perhaps because it was less disruptive to answer than to fend her off, he said, "In the storage room behind the motel. Go through the breezeway."

The three of us hurried along the sidewalk that fronted one wing, toward a gap in the crook of the L. The breezeway held an exterior staircase, an ice machine and a narrow passage to a rear drive that separated the motel from a block wall.

Behind it rose buildings I recognized as belonging to Safe Harbor Community College, which would be virtually empty at this late hour. A fairly safe place to bring a hostage, although Radman was bigger and presumably stronger than Kit Sanchez.

Above the concrete loading dock, a roll-up, garage-style access stood shut. No trucks around, just an old blue sedan.

"That's Kit's car." Brandy hugged herself. "I feel like I'm betraying her."

Tory studied the scene. Nothing obviously amiss, but in the spotty glare of safety lighting, a dark puddle might be oil or blood... or just water. "It's better if I go in there alone."

"I'm a friendly face," the nurse retorted. "She'll react better."

"That might put you in danger."

"We don't know that she's done anything wrong!" Brandy insisted. "I'm going." She forged ahead of us up the steps to the loading dock.

At the top, Tory studied the lock on a normal-size door beside the roll-up. We had no right to break in, I mused. No police authority, no reasonable suspicion of someone in danger, no search warrant.

As my sister-in-law considered her next action, I experienced symptoms I diagnosed as fear: sweating, rapid heartbeat, shortness of breath. Plus anger at myself, for hanging back. Anger at Kit, too, and that jerk Ward, for reducing me to this pathetic state. Which, as a doctor, I knew was perfectly normal.

And, in my opinion, better than false bravado. Safer, anyway.

Tory rapped firmly, a series of thuds. We waited. Maybe no one was home, I thought with a spurt of hope.

Without warning, the door was yanked open. Wild-eyed, Kit wore the same baggy brown sweater as this morning and the same angry twist of the mouth, but those weren't what captured my attention.

That would be the gun in her hand.

"Brandy? What're you doing here?" Her furious gaze swept to Tory. "I know you. You're the cop who arrested me."

She was pointing the gun at us. At me. It was small, but not too small to be lethal. "Who're you?"

My throat got stuck.

"Kit, this is Dr. Darcy, a friend of Alison's," Brandy said. "We're checking on you because..."

"Inside! Now!" The barrel waved, directing us.

When there's a gun aimed at me, I don't see much else. If I were asked to describe the perp to a police artist, I'd be really lousy at it. *She was over twenty-one and under forty. I think she had hair, it might have been brown, and she wasn't very tall.*

We entered a concrete-floored space occupied by metal shelving, bundled linens and boxes of cleaning supplies and paper goods. Nothing sturdy to duck behind, nothing obvious to use as a weapon. On TV, someone would create a distraction so Tory could seize a throwing knife or bolo whip. They didn't appear to stock those in the motel's supply room.

The gun steered us around a row of shelves to a narrow space that held a sprawl of personal possessions and, seated on a sagging couch, a dazed Ward Radman.

Blood oozed from a laceration on his forehead. What had he been hit with, the gun barrel? In the dim light of a pole lamp, I couldn't tell if his pupils were dilated, which might indicate a concussion or drugs.

His wrists and ankles were bound with what appeared to be multiple strands of dental floss. This had not been a well-planned abduction.

"You two, sit," Kit commanded Tory and me. "Brandy, stand next to them. Phones on the floor, and kick them over here."

We obeyed, with me in the middle. She hadn't ordered us to shut them off, which meant we could be tracked. Plus, I had the impression Tory had texted the address to Keith. But without such key words as Gun and Hostage, it could be hours before anyone bothered to look for us.

Tory spoke levelly. "Miss Sanchez, think about what you're doing. Don't go to prison because of what this man did."

As if her crimes didn't already qualify for a bunch of charges. *Keep your mouth shut, Eric.*

"He has to admit he's guilty. To apologize to all the women whose lives he's destroyed." With her left hand, Kit held up her phone, recording video. "Tell the world, you asshole. You raped my sister, Lourdes Sanchez!"

Radman shook his head, with a slight wince. "Don't remember her."

"She was a nurse! She worked with you. You killed her!"

"Didn't kill anybody." A ghost of a smile played around the corners of his mouth. Clinging to the illusion of control. Believing in his superiority.

"You might as well have put the rope around her neck!"

"Kit," Brandy said. "Tory's right. You should stop and think."

188

"Shut up!" Frustrated, the woman was unraveling. I wondered how many bullets she had in that gun and whether, once she started firing, she'd take us all out.

Tory kept her focus on our captor. Gauging the distance and calculating her level of distraction. Or so I presumed.

Beside me, Ward Radman tilted his head. Again, an ugly smile hinted that, despite the danger, he enjoyed Kit's pain. "What do you expect me to say?"

"That you're a rapist and a murderer!" Kit's voice shook with fury. So did the gun in her hand.

"Not true. You're grasping at straws."

"Liar!" The last syllable rose to a shriek. "You murdered Dr. Abrams. Tell the truth!" Any moment, I expected the gun to go off.

Brandy clenched her fists. Swallowing hard, she said, "Kit, Dr. Radman didn't kill Alison."

On my left, Tory stopped studying our abductor to frown at the nurse. "What do you mean?"

"I don't believe she bought those drugs herself," Kit growled.

"Yes, she did," Brandy said. "We planned it."

In the dead silence, I recalled her earlier words. "That's what you meant about this turning into a runaway train."

The nurse nodded grimly. "We wanted vengeance, just like you. Killing him wasn't enough. He had to suffer like we did." After inhaling rapidly, she continued in a strained tone. "We figured the only way to do that was for Alison to rape him."

Even the dust motes stopped wriggling.

Bizarre as it sounded, experiencing that kind of trauma would explain a lot, including the signs of breakdown I'd observed in Radman. In severe cases of PTSD, one's sense of self and ability to reason can collapse. Not his ego, though. Not entirely.

"Ridiculous." His nostrils flared. "We had sex. It was pretty good. I'd give it, oh, about a seven on a scale of ten."

Kit ignored this nasty disrespect toward my dead colleague. "How could she do that?"

"By drugging his drink," Brandy said. "He'd be aware of what was happening but out of control. Helpless, like we were."

"Shut up, you lying slut." Ward leaned forward, so tense he was vibrating. "I'm not some damn victim."

"You shut up, slimebag." Kit's gaze raked me. "Hey, doc. Can a woman rape a man?"

"Yes." While I'm no fan of revenge scenarios, facts are facts. "Our bodies react instinctively to sexual stimulation. And the effects of rape on a man's psyche can be just as profound as on a woman's."

Kit held up her phone. "Got it, doc. The world's gonna love this. Arrogant creep predator Ward Radman got a taste of his own medicine."

With an almost inhuman scream, he jerked to his feet. One step and the dental floss around his ankles snapped.

"You have a problem with rape?" Kit taunted. "That's funny. That's..."

Hands still tied, he plunged toward her across the narrow space, his body nearly blocking my view of her smaller one. His head butted downward, toward hers.

"You son of a—" As Kit stumbled backwards, her arm jerked.

The gun went off.

The boom wasn't nearly as loud as I'd expected. The onrushing form of Dr. Ward Radman served as a very effective muffler.

# CHAPTER TWENTY-THREE

"No!" Radman blurted. It was the final cry from a man whose heart—as I soon discovered—had stopped beating, but whose brain hadn't yet received the message.

He crumpled on top of Kit, and they both collapsed to the floor. Tory bolted for the gun, which had skittered out of Kit's hand.

Brandy snatched up her phone. "Dialing 911," she said, unnecessarily.

Grabbing Ward's limp body, I hauled him off Kit and onto his back, releasing the harsh scent of burnt gunpowder. The young woman lay gasping. "He isn't... is he... I didn't mean to shoot him!"

"Are you okay?" I asked her.

"I wasn't trying to kill him!"

Bending over Ward's body, I spotted a small bullet hole directly over the heart. There was very little blood, even when I tore open his jacket and shirt. No pulse, no breathing. My training kicked in, and I began rapid chest compressions.

"Paramedics and police en route," Brandy told us.

Tory was on her cell, also. "I'm notifying Keith."

Kit sat up, shivering. From the pile of belongings, Brandy

retrieved a blanket to tuck around her. "She doesn't appear injured. Can I help, doc?"

"Afraid not." Although it was clearly useless, I persisted at CPR, with two rescue breaths after every thirty chest compressions. Ward had been shot through the heart. While people have survived that, it's rare.

Brandy hadn't resolved all my questions. This might be my only chance to ask her.

"Why did Alison die?" I panted, short of breath from my labors. "Was that part of the plan?"

"Of course not!" She rested beside Kit, her arm around the stunned woman. "How do you think I felt when I discovered her body in her bathtub? It was worse, worse than anything. Driving her car back to Radman's, I went over and over it in my head, struggling to sort it out."

"Did you succeed?" In the background, I heard Tory—who'd stepped behind a row of shelves—outlining the situation to Keith. Talking faster than usual. Straining to be professional, but shaken, like the rest of us.

"She claimed she was prepared. That she could handle raping him." Tears ran down Brandy's cheeks. Who were they for? Alison? Kit? Surely not Ward Radman, limp beneath my ministrations. "He'd never have admitted being a victim, so we were certain she'd get away with it. We imagined it would change our memories, replace them with a win."

"Why did she take the drugs herself?"

"I don't know! Or why she planted that baggie in his drawer, either. Like she wanted him blamed when.. if..."

"You think she killed herself?" Despite the strain to breathe, I was determined to get as much truth as I could. "You believe raping him brought back the trauma?"

"Maybe she took them to block the pain. Not to die. She wouldn't do this to me!"

Alison had been a doctor, not an impulsive adolescent. "She had to be aware of how much was lethal."

Brandy's shoulders slumped. "I wish wish wish we'd never started this. I'd give anything for a second chance."

"Me, too," Kit whispered.

People say revenge is sweet, but it hadn't been sweet for either of these women. Or for Alison.

One more question struck me. "Why did she have sex with Dr. Schwartz the previous night?"

Brandy blinked. "Oh. That was to prepare."

"Excuse me?"

"Alison never had consensual sex with a man. She wanted the experience. To know how it ought to feel. I thought he'd be a good..." Her voice trailed off.

I bristled on Jeremiah's behalf. "Test subject?"

"Friend."

My arms were tiring. What a relief to hear a siren. I could transfer my patient to the paramedics.

In every other sense, the night's events were just beginning.

\*

Hours later, Tory and I departed after being interviewed at length. Impressions crowded my brain: Ward's lifeless body undergoing futile CPR; a tearful Kit in handcuffs, being checked by paramedics; Keith hugging Tory and scolding her to be more careful; Brandy refusing to talk without an attorney present.

Smart move. There was only her word that she'd helped Alison plan to assault Ward Radman. Although I told the police what I'd heard—as I'm sure Tory did—it occurred to me that Brandy might claim she'd lied. That it had been an effort to persuade Kit that Ward hadn't caused Alison's death, and thus to save his life.

Instead, he'd leaped at an armed captor, daring death

rather than admit the reality of rape. Too bad he had never accepted responsibility for the pain he'd visited on his victims.

The press had swarmed the police station, in a frenzy at learning that Ward Radman was—as he'd finally been declared—dead. I didn't envy Keith's captain, a craggy fellow who'd no doubt been roused from bed to conduct a press conference. He'd released the fact that a young woman had been arrested in conjunction with the celebrity psychiatrist's demise. Everything else was, he'd declared, under investigation.

Amid the commotion, Tory and I had slipped out of the station unnoticed after our interviews. My emotions swung from relief that we were safe to distress at everything that had happened.

At home, as I tipped toward sleep, I was glad Alison had chosen to fight. But her method of doing it was wrong.

Every crime, every evil deed—and every good one as well—sets off a ripple effect. However, unlike water, emotions strengthen as they spread. More of a hurricane effect.

During the next couple of days, newscasts aired an endless stream of details, "expert" opinions and reactions from anyone and everyone. Although Tory and I forbade Morris from watching in our presence, the mutter of smarmy voices sounded whenever his bedroom door opened.

I got off a text to Benjamin about Dr. Radman's death. He responded with several upturned thumbs and a thanks for the information.

At the hospital, I achieved unwanted fame as a witness to the climactic events. The swarm of staffers who peppered me with questions inspired me to eat lunch in my suite's snack room.

"All I care about is that you're safe," my nurse, Farrah, told me as she retrieved her sandwich from the staff fridge.

"Me, too," chimed our young receptionist, dining on take-out. "But, uh, what really went down the night Dr. Abrams died? Was it suicide?"

"Glenda, back off!" Farrah snapped.

"Sorry." As soon as my nurse's attention shifted elsewhere, Glenda rolled her eyes and stuck in her earplugs. Music or news? I couldn't tell.

On Wednesday, the district attorney's office charged Kit Sanchez with first-degree murder. Tory explained that, regardless of whether she'd intended to kill Radman when she kidnapped him, he had died during the commission of a felony.

That evening, Morris insisted on watching Soraya's latest videocast as a condition of sharing his leftover meals with us that evening. We were treated to the information that the charge carried a maximum sentence of twenty-five years to life in prison. Kit's defense counsel, a prominent women's rights attorney, appeared undaunted, claiming that the whole truth had yet to emerge.

I wondered which whole truth she referred to.

Soraya had corralled an analyst to speculate about legal strategies. "Considering that Ms. Sanchez suffered the trauma of finding her sister's body and has been obsessed about seeking what she considers justice for the past dozen years, they could be going for an NGI—not guilty by reason of insanity—defense," the man opined.

As for Brandy Cornello, she was reported to be cooperating with authorities. Although she hadn't been arrested, Tory considered it likely she'd face at least a charge of obstruction of justice.

I was losing my appetite, a rare occurrence. "Isn't there a special on TV about a festival for people who watch cat videos?" I asked.

Morris's eyes flew wide. "That's right. Thanks, Eric."

On Thursday, I again avoided the cafeteria and politely steered my more inquisitive patients to their own circumstances and treatments. Several echoed Farrah's statement that they were grateful I hadn't been harmed.

By six o'clock, my waiting room had emptied and I was preparing to lock up when I had a visitor. Celia Miller, Jeremiah's nurse, slipped into my suite.

"Dr. Darcy?" the red-haired woman greeted me. "I wondered if you could help."

"Of course." Rather odd, though, since she wasn't among my patients.

"I'm worried about Dr. Schwartz."

"What's wrong?" Surely my absence at lunchtime didn't pose a problem, now that Ward's devotees were no longer targeting him. Our administrator's rebuke, coupled with the outspoken support of fellow physicians and the death of their idol, had silenced the loudmouths, Farrah had mentioned.

"I've never seen him this upset." She produced a slightly lopsided smile. "You're the only person he confides in."

Surely he confided in his psychiatrist. But his nurse might not be aware of his mental illness.

Well, I *was* aware of it. He had trusted me with the truth, and now Celia was trusting me to act like a friend. Also, I conceded with a prick of guilt, in avoiding the cafeteria, I'd unintentionally abandoned Jeremiah. "He's still here?"

"Yes."

"Let's go."

Their office lay at the far end of the hall. No patients at this hour, and no staff hanging about, I observed when we entered.

Celia tapped on a partially closed door, then widened it. At a smooth, unnaturally clean desk, beneath stark walls relieved only by framed diplomas, Jeremiah sat staring at his laptop.

His thin face warmed at the sight of me. Something was

different about him... a hint of dark stubble on his cheeks. He'd always been fastidious, and had once confided that he shaved several times per day. "Eric!"

"I'll be off," Celia murmured, and vanished.

"I like the new look," I told Jeremiah.

"I have been experimenting." He rose, rather formally, to shake hands. "I thought you might be angry with me."

"Why on earth?" I pulled up a guest chair. "I've been avoiding the blabbermouths, not you."

He folded himself onto his chair. "Should I have called? I am no longer sure how to behave, since I have resolved not to pattern myself after you."

"That doesn't mean we can't talk," I said, although I doubted anything I could share would improve Jeremiah's spirits. However, there's another misguided popular saying: The truth hurts. Well, lies hurt more.

"I have emotions that are irrational," Jeremiah said. "You may understand them better than I."

"Shoot."

"Well..." His hesitation before continuing was uncharacteristic. Celia had been right; he was upset. "I have heard stories circulating about Alison. The consensus is that she brought drugs to Ward Radman's house and chose to commit suicide."

"That appears to be the case," I said.

"None of these stories explain why she visited me the previous night, or how that affected her." His dark eyes fixed on me, as if I held the secrets of the universe. "Did sex with me push her over the edge? Was she so distraught that she sought comfort from Ward Radman and killed herself when that failed?"

Good lord, he'd been tormenting himself over this? "No," I said.

"You cannot be certain."

"Actually, I can."

I related Brandy's confession: the planned revenge, the drugs, the likelihood that Alison's trauma had overwhelmed her. And the preparation, taking into account that she'd never had consensual sex.

"I was practice?" he asked.

"She chose you as a man she trusted," I said. "Unfortunately, she didn't behave in a trustworthy manner toward you. No one deserves to be used sexually."

I awaited his reaction.

He stared into space. Then: "Your statement implies that sex with me provided the strength for her to even the score with Radman. I am sorry it was not more unpleasant."

"Pardon?" Although he had a right to be resentful, it seemed out of character.

"If our encounter had aroused bad memories, she might not have gone through with it," he pointed out. "She could still be alive."

He wasn't resentful; he was generous. "Adults are responsible for their own decisions. However damn stupid they may be."

"Would you say the same of Lydia?" he asked.

As Chava had mentioned, I'd spent the better part of three years immersed in anger, regret, and sorrow. Then I'd stood on a mountaintop and released those emotions, save for the echoes that would always stay with me.

"For a long time, I thought I had failed her," I said. "Maybe we failed each other, but in the end, it was her choice."

"A stupid one?" he asked.

"To die alone, guarding fears and secrets that should have been shared?" I said. "In my opinion, yes."

"I have another question."

"Okay." I wasn't feeling much like a font of wisdom, though.

"Regarding secrets," Jeremiah said. "I am relieved to have told you and Detective Sparks that I am schizophrenic. I am unsure, however, whether to impart this information to others."

"Which others?"

He shrugged. "Others in general."

Sharing secrets does not require blabbing them to an often irrational public. "Is it affecting your practice of medicine?"

"I do not believe so," he said.

"I wouldn't share my personal diagnosis as long as it didn't harm patients," I responded.

His shoulders relaxed. "Thank you. Is it acceptable if sometimes I continue to use you as a touchstone?"

"I'd be honored." I rose, and we shook hands.

As for Lydia, I had one more task to accomplish. It played through my mind all the way home.

# CHAPTER TWENTY-FOUR

Once upon a time, nine years ago, a man and a woman who had dated since early adolescence walked up a flower-bedecked aisle together, hand in hand. Later that day, we posed for a photo in the company of our closest companions.

During my marriage, the framed picture had hung in our master bedroom. After Lydia's death, squeezed unbearably by the sight of my former happiness, I transferred it into the guest room.

Standing in front of it now, I had the impression that all light focused on the bride. Petite and dainty, Lydia Silver Darcy wore her almost-black hair arranged in long, loose curls above the rainbow-hued dress she herself had designed.

Her mouth quirked in a mysterious smile, which I had later attempted to analyze and interpret. Was she missing her mother, who had died five years earlier? Had she held doubts about our marriage? Or was she simply tired from a long day?

How young we looked: Keith, Lydia's brother Barry, and me in our tuxedos; Tory towering over her half-sister and, on her far side, Lydia's friend Shana. As I recalled, we'd been eager to finish posing and join the celebration, never imagining how the future would fling us about in its current.

But the six of us hadn't been the only ones in that picture. We carried our ancestors inside us, the genes, the joys and the traumas handed down to us. The secrets, too.

Most of us can't and shouldn't face the future alone, especially when pain overwhelms us. I believe everyone has the power to heal, ourselves and others. By caring. By listening. By exploring the truth about our past but refusing to let it define us.

When it's bad enough, either it drives us to despair or we work through it, one step at a time. While I no longer doubted that Lydia had loved me, she'd turned inward when she should have reached out.

There is no statute of limitations on grief, but there should be. Finally, I was ready to lay my wife to rest and move forward.

Someday I might even fall in love again. Now, there was a scary thought.

The End

The Beginning

# ABOUT THE AUTHOR

A former Associated Press reporter and TV columnist, *USA Today* bestselling author Jacqueline Diamond has sold more than one hundred novels. These include mysteries, medical romances, Regency romances and romantic comedies published by Harlequin, St. Martin's Press, William Morrow and Five Star Mysteries, among others. Jackie and her husband live in Southern California.

Jackie is best known for her Safe Harbor Medical romances and mysteries. Among the titles are *The Case of the Questionable Quadruplet, The Case of the Surly Surrogate, The Case of the Desperate Doctor* and *The Case of the Long-Lost Lover.*

You can sign up for her free newsletter and learn more about her books at her website, www.jacquelinediamond.net.

If you enjoyed this novel and are willing to post a short review at your favorite online book sites, it would be much appreciated. Thank you!

www.ingramcontent.com/pod-product-compliance
Lightning Source LLC
Chambersburg PA
CBHW020115180626
46812CB00006B/2607